**"I'm to blame."**

Cat started. "You? Why would you say that?"

"'Tis the McKennas' lot to lose the people they care about."

He cared about her? Her pulse quickened. "I don't understand."

"'Tis a curse."

She listened to his story about how the witch, Sheelin O'Keefe, had cursed Donal McKenna's progeny to put their loved ones in mortal danger.

"You believe in a psychic connection with your horses," Cat said. "And now a witch's curse."

"You think I am making all this up?" He sounded upset.

"It makes a good story."

"'Tis all true!" Aidan argued. "My family has lost too many loved ones to think otherwise."

"Everyone loses someone they care about."

"But not always the person who is their soul mate."

# PATRICIA ROSEMOOR

# PUREBRED

TORONTO NEW YORK LONDON
AMSTERDAM PARIS SYDNEY HAMBURG
STOCKHOLM ATHENS TOKYO MILAN MADRID
PRAGUE WARSAW BUDAPEST AUCKLAND

Thanks to my cousins Carol Morrison and MaryAnn Pusz for spending a fun day helping me get the background I needed for this story.



ISBN-13: 978-0-373-74666-8

PUREBRED



This edition published by arrangement with Harlequin Books S.A.

For questions and comments about the quality of this book please contact us at Customer_eCare@Harlequin.ca.



www.Harlequin.com

**Printed in U.S.A.**

## ABOUT THE AUTHOR

Patricia Rosemoor has always had a fascination with dangerous love. She loves bringing a mix of thrills and chills and romance to Harlequin Intrigue readers. She's won a Golden Heart from Romance Writers of America and a Reviewers' Choice and Career Achievement Awards from *RT Book Reviews*. She teaches courses on writing popular fiction and suspense-thriller writing in the fiction writing department of Columbia College Chicago. Check out her website, www.PatriciaRosemoor.com. You can contact Patricia either via email at Patricia@PatriciaRosemoor.com, or through the publisher at Patricia Rosemoor, c/o Harlequin Books, 233 Broadway, New York, NY 10279.

## Books by Patricia Rosemoor

HARLEQUIN INTRIGUE

707—VIP PROTECTOR‡
745—BOYS IN BLUE
"Zachary"
785—VELVET ROPES‡
791—ON THE LIST‡
858—GHOST HORSE
881—RED CARPET CHRISTMAS‡
924—SLATER HOUSE
958—TRIGGERED RESPONSE
1031—WOLF MOON*
1047—IN NAME ONLY?*
1101—CHRISTMAS DELIVERY
1128—RESCUING THE VIRGIN*
1149—STEALING THUNDER*
1200—SAVING GRACE*
1261—BRAZEN*
1292—DEAL BREAKER*
1345—PUREBRED*

‡Club Undercover
*The McKenna Legacy

## CAST OF CHARACTERS

***Aidan McKenna***—The Irish horse trainer has already lost one woman to the McKenna curse.

***Cat (Catrina) Clarke***—The breeder puts everything she has left at risk to form a partnership with Aidan.

***George Odell***—The barn manager mysteriously disappeared while Cat was in Ireland.

***Raul Ayala***—What would the barn worker do to make certain Aidan and Cat hired his jockey brother?

***Tim Browne***—What is the hotwalker hiding?

***Dean Hill***—What would the horse owner do to own another champion?

***Bernie Hansen***—The barn worker with an attitude seems to be around every time something bad happens.

***Jack Murray***—Cat's ex-husband betrayed and cheated her, but could he be guilty of worse?

***Martin Bradley***—Is the horse owner willing to back Cat's ex no matter the consequences?

***Dr. Ellen Fox***—Does the vet know what's happening in Cat's barn at night?

June 22, 1919

Donal McKenna,
Ye might have found happiness with another woman, but yer progeny will pay for this betrayal of me. I call on my faerie blood and my powers as a witch to give yers only sorrow in love, for should they act on their feelings, they will put their loved ones in mortal danger.

So be it,
Sheelin O'Keefe

## *Prologue*

Lightning split the sky and the man ran as fast as he could, his feet slipping and sliding on the sodden pasture grass.

Damn! Why did it have to be tonight of all nights? The rain was incessant.

So much depended on getting this right. Maybe a couple million dollars much.

He'd parked on a side road and had come the back way so as not to be seen, but each lightning strike hit the area like a giant lamp. By the time he got into the barn, where the horses rumbled their displeasure at the storm, his heart was thundering and his chest squeezed tight. Might think he was having a heart attack if the bundle he carried didn't weigh a ton.

"Thought you weren't coming."

Words assailing him from the dark were followed by his partner stepping out of the shadows into the dimly lit aisle.

"Have you taken a look outside lately?" Though

he felt like jumping out of his skin, it wouldn't do to let the man see him sweat. Still, he gladly gave over the package he'd carried from the car. "You sure you know how to do this?"

The other man nodded. "Not rocket science."

He didn't argue that it was close. They had to get this right. It had to work.

Everything looked well-prepared. His partner had even mucked out the stall. The tools and wheelbarrow stood next to the open stall door. But watching the other man prepare for the procedure, he went all jittery inside.

How long was this going to take?

What if someone walked in on them before they finished?

"Hurry up!" he growled.

His partner in crime paused to give him a dark look. "You want this done fast or you want it done right?"

"Okay, okay!"

He would do it himself if he could. Trying to calm down, he paced the length of the aisle, his mere presence setting off more nickering and snorting. Dark eyes turned on him, as if the horses were accusing him before the men even got started.

At least the animals couldn't talk.

When this night's work was done, he *would* be guilty of a serious crime.

*No guilt,* he told himself, as his partner finally got down to business. Chewing some antacids to calm his boiling stomach, he watched with fascination. It was just what needed to be done. He wouldn't let it eat at him. Wouldn't even think about it.

Not until next time.

Suddenly the overhead lights flashed on and the barn glowed from within and a rough voice called out. "Hey, what're you doing there?"

The barn manager, who wasn't scheduled to work tonight, had shown up anyway.

Bile rose in his throat.

"Got a sick horse," he said, sliding his hand along the stall door until he found a tool he could use. Moving forward toward the unexpected intruder, he knew what he had to do, no getting around it.

The older man stopped and from the end of the aisle assessed the situation. He frowned. "Sick? With what?"

"With this!" he said, leaping forward, striking out and hitting the man's head with a mucking shovel.

The manager went down like a sack of feed.

"What the hell'd you do?" his partner demanded.

"What I had to." His stomach churned. *No guilt,*

he reminded himself. He wouldn't even think about it after tonight. "Now finish so we can clean up this mess."

## *Chapter One*

*County Galway, Ireland*

"Pegeen would have loved to ride you," Aidan McKenna said past the lump in his throat as he led Mac Finnian into his stall after his morning workout and cooldown.

Mac snorted and pranced in his stall, ready to run again.

Indeed, Aidan could read him, had been able to do so since the black colt was born. He'd always had a connection with the horses he trained—he was a McKenna, after all—even if that particular ability was less developed than that of his brothers. He, instead, wrestled with dreams and nightmares, trying to decide which were true portents of the future and which were figments of his overwrought imagination. Sadly, he didn't always get it right. But he didn't want to think on it now—didn't want to remember his tragic mistake with Pegeen.

Instead he concentrated on the strong connection he had with Mac, the only McKenna ability welcome in life. 'Twas almost as if they were one.

Aidan removed the lead and then unfastened Mac's halter and slipped it off his big head. Everything about the colt was big—he stood a bit more than seventeen hands, nearly a full hand larger than the average Thoroughbred. Thankfully, even the smallest jockeys were flexible enough to sit his broad back.

Aidan could almost see Mac running in the Irish Derby, the woman he'd loved with her shocking red hair and bold ways atop the black colt. Pegeen would have been grinning from ear to ear as she eagerly raced him. But of course now that could never happen.

From her grave, Sheelin O'Keefe had seen to that.

Despite his brother Cashel's dire warnings, Aidan had taken up with the Irish jockey, and Sheelin's curse had ended Pegeen Flynn's life before she'd had a chance to really live.

After the better part of a year without her, still mourning the only woman he'd ever cared for, he was wondering if the pain of losing Pegeen would ever subside when Cashel entered the stable, followed by the dark-haired lass he'd seen watching Mac's run with his brother. She was a looker—a natural beauty with lush curves. Not wanting his brother to realize where his mind had wandered a moment ago, Aidan immediately tucked away his thoughts for later. For when he was alone.

Giving Mac a peppermint, he shut the stall door behind him and stared at the light in his older brother's eyes, the same McKenna-green as both his own and their younger brother Tiernan's. The three McKenna men looked alike, too, all tall, broad-shouldered, with thick dark hair brushing chiseled features. Today, Cashel's were softened into something that looked like hope.

"Aidan, our problems are solved!" Cashel said. "This is Catrina Clarke from America. We can have the backing we need to race Mac there."

But Aidan didn't have reason to trust hope. "And what kind of backing is it you offer from America, Miss Clarke?"

"Call me Cat. I'm a breeder and I came to Ireland on a buying trip, to add new blood to my stock. But when I saw Mac Finnian run..."

Her breath caught in her throat and Aidan's caught in his. It wasn't just her natural beauty, but something in her voice—something that told him she was more than a businesswoman when it came to fine horseflesh—that seduced him.

Just for a moment.

Then he shook himself free.

"Out with it, then," he said.

"I know you don't have the funds to race him

in the U.S., and I'm willing to make a deal so that will be possible." Her smile widened, lighting up her whole face.

Once again, he was caught by the fire that burned within her.

Until the colt kicked the stall door for attention. Mac had hung his head into the aisle and now snorted at his owners. Aidan reached back and scratched the sweet spot on his long, muscular neck before turning his attention back to his brother.

"We're not selling anyone half interest in our colt!"

"But that's not the deal I offered!" the woman protested.

Knowing he had to get away from the Clarke woman before he caved, Aidan snorted and headed for the exit. Cashel followed and Aidan realized the lass had chosen to remain where she was. He took a good look back. There she stood, her back stiff, her mouth now in a straight line. And then her cell phone rang and after a glance at her screen, she frowned and wandered off to take the call in private.

"Of course I wouldn't agree to sell," Cashel said, grabbing his arm and stopping him from leaving. "The Clarke woman wanted to buy Mac outright, but I told her that wasn't possible. What kind of sodding fool do you take me for?"

"So what are her plans for Mac Finnian?"

"She simply offered a very fair partnership. She'll not own any of Mac, simply get a share in the winnings until we retire him from—"

"How much, then?"

"A third."

Aidan gaped at his brother. "'Tis ridiculous!" he shouted.

Cashel raised his voice, as well. "You want to give it up, then, just stay here and run him on Irish grass?"

Looking out through the open door into the misting rain and the emerald green pastures beyond the barn, Aidan wanted to say the colt would do well enough, but he knew "well enough" would be a disappointment to them both. The previous September, Mac had won a couple of Group 2 races by a nose but had only come in second in the Group 1 stakes race at the Curragh and had come in third in another.

In a country where races were run on grass like that which stretched on forever before him, they'd bred a colt who wanted to run on dirt. A colt who ran like the wind on dirt. A colt who could *win big* on dirt.

But it wouldn't be here or in any country close by.

The logical thing was to race Mac where he would run best, and that would be in the United

States. There Mac Finnian could race on dirt tracks.

"Think about it, Aidan. He could advance to the Breeders' Cup Classic with an honest chance of becoming a world champion."

And if that happened as they both thought it could, at last McKenna Racing would earn the reputation it needed. Then they would have their pick of top-flight racehorses to train.

But the only way they could race Mac in America without selling parts of him off was to take the deal. And take the woman with it. He shook his head. Something deep inside was telling him this was a bad idea. A very bad idea.

"We're nearly broke and you know it, Aidan," Cashel continued. "The stud fees to get Mac and the fees to nominate him for the Breeders' Cup ate up our savings, and the horses we've been training haven't exactly had a grand year."

True, those fees had totaled six figures. Plus their share of winnings this year had been slim enough that Aidan feared losing owners who might not keep faith in them to train their Thoroughbreds to be champions.

When Aidan still didn't say anything, Cashel went on. "You know the cost of flying Mac Finnian internationally, quarantining him and setting him up in a foreign barn—not to mention the racing entry fees—well, that's more money than we've seen in too long a time."

Aidan knew that as well as his brother. Realizing he would have to consider the offer as much as he hated to admit it, he relented. "Mac'll never be the best he can be racing here. We do need to consider the partnership."

"There are another couple caveats to which we must agree."

"And those would be?"

"The Clarke woman gets a third of his stud fees for the first year. And she gets to use him at stud on her own mares with no fee. One live foal per mare, an even half dozen. That was the price of not selling a share in him outright. Apparently she wants to expand her business. I'm thinking she might want to get into racing in the future, as well."

If so, Aidan couldn't blame her. Thoroughbred racing fueled his blood. And his dreams. Dreams that, under the proper conditions, Mac could make come true.

"I don't like her setting the terms, though," Aidan muttered, thinking she was likely to get under his skin the moment he saw her again. Attraction warred with irritation. He didn't need either. As if she'd heard him via some mental connection, she was stalking toward them now, her face wreathed in an angry thundercloud. "If only there was another way."

"You know there is. We could syndicate the colt, then."

"And divide him up into little pieces?" He glared at Cashel. He knew his brother didn't want that any more than he did. It was simply Cashel's annoying attempt at getting his way. Cursing under his breath, Aidan said, "All right, then."

"Grand! Don't worry, I'll see that Mac will be well taken care of."

Aidan started. "What does that mean?"

"Just what it sounds like. I look forward to the American races."

As usual, Cashel was trying to take over as if he were Aidan's boss rather than his partner in the business. The curse of having a sometimes autocratic older brother…

"You'll be doing no such thing." Knowing it was time he made his own mark, Aidan stood his ground. "*I'm* the one who trained Mac practically from the time he was foaled, not you. I'm the one who will be taking our colt to America."

Truth to tell, Aidan would be glad to get away from his overbearing brother for a while. Noting the smirk Cashel quickly hid, he wondered if he'd been tricked into volunteering.

Seeing that Cat was standing there like a stone-cold statue, obviously tuned in to their disagreement, he ground out, "To where exactly?" Even if Cashel had tricked him, Aidan wouldn't back up now. Mac Finnian was *his* responsibility. "Kentucky? New York? California?"

"My farm is in Woodstock, Illinois."

"The Midwest?" He knew Cashel had been in the area once before for the Arlington Million, while Aidan had stayed behind to tend to the other horses they were training. "That would be in the middle of nowhere!"

"As if this is the only somewhere," Cat said. "Get over yourself, McKenna. There are places in the world other than your little patch of green. I can provide the means for you to see them, but I need to catch the next flight out. I've been called home for an unexpected court date. And my barn manager has done a disappearing act—" Catching herself before going on, she took a big breath and looked him squarely in the face. "When you decide what you want to do, call me."

With that, she headed straight for the exit.

Cashel laughed. "At least Cat Clarke is something to look at."

Aidan found no fault with her looks—she was indeed fair, with a small waist and full hips and dark hair that teased breasts lush enough to tempt a man—it was the lass herself and the attraction that stirred his guilt that created the problem.

"I'm going to town to pick up some supplies," he said stiffly.

"If you have no further objections, I'll make the arrangements, then," Cashel said. "I assume your agreement stands."

"Do what you need to."

Striding out of the barn into the soft day, where a fine, light mist covered him like fairy dust, Aidan wondered what he was getting himself into. Cat Clarke had come to Galway on an equine buying trip and had been sidetracked to watch Mac Finnian run on a practice dirt track, where she'd apparently been overly impressed with his time.

While he'd been overly impressed with her until she'd taken that call. Her snapping at him was enough to convince him that he'd do best to stay away from her. She had a temper, that one, and she had attitude that reminded him of Cashel. Always one to be in charge.

He preferred his women easy-going and good-natured, and Catrina Clarke was the complete opposite. Put her with himself and they were like oil and water.

Facts were facts, though. They'd had no better offer.

Mac Finnian wasn't just any horse. He wasn't simply a commodity to either McKenna brother and especially not to Aidan, who'd connected with him on a whole different level from the moment he'd been born. If he wanted to give Mac a chance to restore their coffers and make McKenna Racing's name as top trainers in the Thoroughbred industry—and all without giving up ownership of the colt—he had no choice in the matter.

Truth be told, Aidan needed a change, needed to get away from the familiar. Needed to get away from Cashel. He hoped the change in venue would be as good for him as it would be for Mac Finnian.

Maybe getting away from Galway would free him from the dreams that haunted him, the guilt and memories of how their troubles had really begun.

Of how the only woman he'd ever loved had died.

Because of him.

*He hadn't had sex in too many moons. Any time he'd thought of it, memories of Pegeen had stopped him.*

*And now he couldn't stop himself.*

*He was in her, touching her, making her moan. The sound vibrated through him, all the way to the length of flesh buried deep inside her.*

*They were both panting...moving frantically... her full flesh butting his hips...trying to achieve something elusive...something just out of reach.*

*Her back was to him so he couldn't see her face,*

*but her dark hair spilling down her back teased him with its sensuous softness and scent.*

*He ran his tongue up her arm to her neck and lightly bit the soft flesh cradling her shoulder. She cried out and he felt himself give way, imagined tumbling over and over and over a waterfall until he sagged against her in glorious defeat...*

Aidan woke with a start. He'd soiled his sheets with the first sexual relief he'd experienced since the funeral.

"No, no, no!"

Pegeen had not been the woman he could still see in his mind's eye.

He hadn't seen her face, but the woman had long dark hair like Catrina Clarke.

Could he trust the dream or not?

He no longer knew.

Either he'd had a peek into the future, or he'd been tricked again.

Either way it didn't bode well for his new partnership.

He had to make sure the dream didn't take on a life of its own this time.

## *Chapter Two*

*Woodstock, Illinois*

"So what do you think?" Cat asked, when the vet finished examining Diamond Dame, one of her biggest client's broodmares.

Helen Fox removed her examination gloves and disposed of them. "I think she'll be ready for cover in a few days. Make sure you tease her with a stallion between now and then since she's a maiden."

"Got it." Cat grinned at the redhead. "Things are going so well, I can't help thinking this is going to be a spectacular breeding season."

"You're good at what you do. That's why I like working with you."

Cat liked Helen, as well. The vet loved her job. Loved animals. In her early forties, trim and attractive enough to look far younger, undoubtedly because her job so agreed with her.

Cat followed the vet out of the barn. "More mares will be coming in to be bred next week."

"I'll be back tomorrow to see if Diamond Dame is ready. And to check on Fairy Tail."

"Hopefully she'll be with foal," Cat joked.

When she caught sight of the shiny new red truck pulling up in her drive, Cat felt her pulse immediately jump. It wasn't that seeing her ex-husband excited her. Quite the opposite.

Helen got into her truck and started the engine. "If you get three out of three of Dean's mares on the first try, he'll have to buy us a bottle of champagne to celebrate."

Cat waved the vet goodbye, a smile now plastered to her face. She was going to have to deal with Jack. Knowing he'd come because he wanted something from her, she was on edge at his very presence. She didn't wait for him to swagger over to her.

Leaving the barking dogs locked in the house, she met him halfway to the truck. He'd bought the shiny new toy with money he'd demanded and gotten from her in the divorce settlement. Beneath a tousle of wheat-blond hair, his gray eyes lit with amusement and his thin lips stretched into a smile, both of which made her cringe inside.

"What is it this time, Jack?" she asked. "Could there possibly be something you forgot to take from me?"

He'd already taken her self-respect, in addition to money he hadn't earned and several of her best mares, to boot. She'd been grateful the judge had allowed her to hang on to her stallion. The farm itself was a Clarke family land trust, so thankfully Jack hadn't been able to lay his sticky fingers on any part of it.

"Now, Cat, is that any way to talk to the man you love?" he asked.

He moved closer so she had to look up at him.

"If I ever loved you, Jack, I can't remember. You drove any good feelings out of me long ago."

"Is that your excuse—?"

"I need no excuse for anything where you're concerned. You lost the right to my good will when you took up with that..." She wanted to say *that bimbo,* but she bit it back since the other woman's father was still a good client. "...woman."

"You mean my fiancée."

"Now you're marrying her?"

"Of course I am. I can't live without her. We're getting married as soon as possible."

The snide note in her ex-husband's tone rankled. Though they'd lived apart for the better part of a year, more than half as long as they'd been together, the divorce had only been finalized a few weeks before. To her shock, she'd been summoned back from her buying trip in Ireland for a final court date. Jack hadn't been able to wait to openly be with Simone Bradley.

Simone obviously didn't see Jack for the cheater and liar that he really was. He was good, really good, at fooling people. Women. Her. Undoubtedly Jack considered Simone a step up and had somehow convinced the young woman that he'd been the injured party in the marriage.

"As soon as possible?" Cat asked, unable to keep the sarcasm from her voice. "Is it because she's pregnant?"

"Would you be jealous if she was?"

"No, although I'm sure you would like that. The only blessing in our marriage is that I never brought a poor child into this world."

"Another reason I left you."

Cat swallowed hard and didn't respond. She wouldn't let him see how it bothered her. At thirty, she was completely aware of her biological clock. Being a breeder made her doubly aware of the irony of not conceiving herself. When Cat had learned of Jack's affair, she'd felt like a fool, and had tried to see the positive side of not having children. Betrayed by the man she'd loved, Cat had not only thrown his ring back at him but his name, as well. She'd since done her best to get Jack Murray out of her life forever.

But here he was again, on her doorstep.

What would he demand of her this time?

"I have work to do. Whatever it is, make it fast."

"I hear you're backing an Irish colt, bringing him here to race, paying the entry fees. Thousands upon thousands of dollars."

"Which is none of your business."

"That's big bucks. Obviously, you were hiding assets."

"I'm not the liar here, Jack. You are."

"Give me my cut and I won't take you back to court." Jack's demand was muted by the sound of another vehicle pulling up.

Cat looked past him to see her horse trailer being driven in by Raul Ayala, one of her workers. The Irish colt in question had arrived. Why now of all times? She'd waited anxiously for the two weeks it had taken to run blood tests to make sure the colt was healthy, then days while he'd been quarantined in New York. Ironic that Jack had to ruin his highly anticipated arrival…just as he'd ruined so many things for her.

Jack looked, too, and then grinned at her. "Maybe I should talk to your new partner—"

"Jack, just get off my property. Now!"

"You can't kick me out, Cat. If I give Martin the word, he'll pull his broodmares and stallion from your barn, and where will that leave you?"

Cat gaped. He might be able to do it, too, since apparently he was going to be Martin Bradley's son-in-law.

"It might be worth it to get you out of my life once and for all!"

Although it might break her financially. And she'd always gotten along with Martin, if not with his daughter Simone.

Aidan McKenna jumped out of the passenger seat of the truck, and with a terse nod at her, went around back to check on the colt. Her stomach clenched. She didn't want him embroiled in the middle of her troubles with her ex-husband. Not a pretty way to start a business partnership.

"I see George hasn't returned," Jack noted, as if he hadn't just dropped a bomb on her. "What did you do to chase *him* away?" He made it sound like it had been her fault that he'd strayed from their marriage bed.

Cat went speechless for a moment.

Apparently right after she'd left for Ireland, George Odell had simply disappeared. No one claimed to have seen him since. He'd worked for her family since he was a young man. She couldn't fathom his leaving without giving her some good reason—not to mention a way to contact him—and feared something bad had happened to the old man. The fact that most of his things were still in his trailer didn't mean anything to the authorities, because it was obvious he'd packed a bag—some of his clothes, his good boots and his shaving kit were gone. According to the police, it wasn't a crime or a reason for concern for a man to leave his job without notice, not even if he didn't collect his back pay.

Cat only hoped they were right, and that one day George would simply show up with an explanation as to why he'd had to leave for a while.

"You owe me money, Cat. If you used up your cash on him," Jack said, indicating Aidan, "I'll settle for a couple more broodmares."

A statement that made Cat go stiff. "You already got your settlement in court."

"I'm going to give those broodmares I was awarded to Simone as a wedding gift. Martin will want you to breed them, of course."

Cat gaped at him. "You bastard!"

During the divorce settlement, she'd learned how greedy he could be, but she hadn't known he could be this cruel.

"Go to your new woman if you need cash!"

"What I need is the cash to buy her an engagement ring that will turn heads."

Cat held herself in tight control so that she wouldn't lash out at the bastard. She wanted to slap him—hard!—in the worst way. If only she could get him out of her life. If only she could. Him and Simone. The young woman often came to Clarke Acres with her father, Martin, to check on his broodmares.

"What did you do with the settlement, Jack?

More bad investments? Don't come to me to solve your problems!" Realizing she was yelling, she reined in her temper the best she could. "And stop threatening me. Now, get off my property before I call the sheriff!"

With that, she stalked away from him, chest heaving, unable to take a normal breath as she approached the truck and horse trailer. Now she had to deal with another man in the racing game who set her on edge, but she couldn't let him get to her.

She had to make nice to her new partner.

She'd taken a loan to get the money to bring Mac Finnian from Ireland, and since she didn't own the farm outright, she'd used her broodmares as collateral. Her business and future was riding on this relationship.

When she heard Jack's truck start up and move off, Cat was relieved. The last thing she needed was for Jack to complicate things for her right now.

She had to prove herself.

If Mac really was as good as she thought he was, he'd race only a year or two at the most, and then be put to stud for six-figure fees. She would pay back the loan with her percentage of the money he made. Then she would be able to breed him with her mares and hopefully foal the next generation of Illinois Thoroughbred champions. Whether she sold the colts and fillies or raced them herself was the big bonus, the opportunity to have money in the bank again, to enhance her reputation, to expand her business—all reasons she'd taken this chance.

As Aidan jumped out of the back of the trailer, she tried to assure herself this wasn't impossible, tried not to be affected by his bigger-than-life presence. That had been the first thing she'd noticed about him when they'd been introduced in Ireland.

The hitch was that she would have to work with Aidan to make the farm's success happen. Having heard the argument between him and his brother, she feared getting along with him would be as difficult as dealing with Jack.

No, he couldn't possibly be as infuriating as her ex-husband.

Although the way Aidan was looking at her now, caution stilling his perfectly chiseled features, his thick-lashed green eyes narrowing on her, Cat knew she had her work cut out for her.

She had to make this partnership succeed.

*Had to,* or she could lose everything.

## *Chapter Three*

"Welcome to Clarke Acres, Aidan," Cat said, holding out her hand.

He took it for a shake and was surprised both by her strength and the feel of her palm and fingers. No softness there. It was evident she didn't just run the place but worked it herself. She was dressed in dirt-streaked work clothes—cotton shirt rolled to the elbows, jeans, mucking boots—and her dark hair was pulled back from her makeup-free face in a ponytail. Not that she needed makeup or a fancy hairdo or clothes. She was attractive without trying.

"To the start of a successful partnership," he said.

"I'm counting on it."

Though her words were positive, her smile was forced and didn't quite reach her hazel eyes. Because of the argument she'd just had with the ex, or because of him? He'd known she had a temper, so while mildly unpleasant, witnessing the argument had been no surprise.

Aidan nodded and released her hand. “Where does Mac go, then?”

She indicated the very large building set back a hundred yards from the house. “Raul will get him set up in a stall.”

“I’ll be doing that myself, if you don’t mind.”

“Oh…of course. I just thought you might be tired from the flight. Or hungry.”

The flight from Shannon to New York had exhausted him, but he’d had three days to recuperate while the colt had been quarantined. The two-hour flight from New York to Chicago had raced by in comparison. But they didn’t feed him in economy, and then, after the plane had landed, he’d been too concerned with checking to make sure Mac had made a safe crossing to worry about finding food for himself.

“I could use a bit of food,” he admitted. “After I make sure the colt is settled.”

Cat nodded. “I don’t cook fancy, but I have a pot roast in the Crock-Pot. It’ll be ready anytime you are.” She moved to the front of the trailer and opened the truck’s passenger door. “Raul, please take them to the barn, and show Mr. McKenna around. Get him anything he needs.” She indicated Aidan should get back in the passenger seat.

"Then bring him around to the house and take his bags down the rear stairs."

"Yes, ma'am."

Aidan nodded as he climbed back into the truck. Cat had thought of everything, including a temporary living arrangement in something called an in-law apartment on the lower level of her home. He would make certain that it would be very temporary. Once he settled Mac in a stable at the track, he would then look for a flat for himself nearby. Confident he could control what did or did not happen between them if he put his mind to it, Aidan knew he couldn't chance living this close to Cat for any length of time.

As Raul drove to the far end of the barn, Aidan noticed an outdoor arena and four paddocks. "So how big is the farm?"

"Seventeen acres."

"What about the barn?"

"Forty-two twelve-by-twelve-foot box stalls, nearly a dozen empty right now," Raul said. "But it's still early in the breeding season. In the next week or two, owners will be lined up to get their broodmares in and out of here, and then there won't be enough room."

"So she has a good stallion."

"Good enough, I guess. He's loco sometimes. Dangerous, like his name."

Raul's lack of enthusiasm confirmed Cat's

reason for wanting to get Mac Finnian at stud. His sire lines were impeccable—Mr. Prospector and Bold Ruler before that—as were the dam's sire lines—Sadler's Wells and before him Alleged.

"What else is in the main barn?" Aidan asked.

"There's two foaling stalls with video feeds to the house, an indoor arena, two tack rooms, office, laundry and medicine room."

"Impressive place."

"Miss Clarke does okay for herself."

Though it should have sounded like a compliment, Aidan sensed something else there. Resentment? Maybe Raul didn't like working for a woman but didn't have a choice. Aidan took a better look at the worker. The man was small but muscular and had bronzed features that were smooth but for the wrinkles around his dark eyes. Aidan guessed him to be nearing forty or so. Wondering how long Raul had worked here, but wanting to know more about the farm and Cat, he decided to keep his own counsel until he got to know the man better. Raul hadn't said much since they'd loaded Mac into the trailer, had only spoken when necessary.

As Raul slowed near a back door, Aidan could see another building farther back on the property, no doubt to hold equipment and supplies. And opposite the buildings, three large four-board fenced pastures and a small dirt track. The farm wasn't as green as the countryside in Ireland, but it was far more so than he'd been expecting. Far more extensive, too.

Cat Clarke was indeed doing okay for herself, which made Aidan feel better about his situation. He got out of the truck and went around to unload Mac from the trailer. She was a seasoned professional and would undoubtedly do everything in her power to help him make the colt into a champion.

So why did he have the niggling feeling that everything wasn't as it seemed?

WHILE AIDAN WAS GETTING the colt settled, Cat took the opportunity to shower. She'd bred Fairy Tail, one of Dean Hill's broodmares, that morning and hadn't had a chance to clean up and do something with her hair. Her sprucing up had nothing to do with wanting to impress Aidan McKenna, at least not in a personal way. She hoped to appear the successful businesswoman she wished she really was so that he would have confidence in their new partnership.

Imagining what he might have thought coming in on her fight with her ex-husband, she quickly blow-dried her hair, then entered the bedroom where her two dogs, Smokey and Topaz, were waiting for her with hopeful gazes.

"All right. Give me a second." As she fetched

treats from a container on her dresser, they pushed into her legs. “Go get it.” She tossed the treats across the room and smiled when the dogs bounded after them.

She loved this room that had been hers since childhood. It was all grown up now, with pale gold walls and cranberry and gold bedding. Her favorite thing, though, was the wall holding a smattering of framed photos that traced her history—her on her first pony, her with the horse she’d ridden at her first competition with the ribbon she’d won attached to the frame, her with the first mare she’d bred. And of course the family photos—Mom, Dad, her brother Jens. And George. While not blood kin, she’d always thought of him as an honorary uncle.

Thinking about his disappearance threatened to bring her down again, so she shifted direction. She hadn’t made a great first impression on Aidan. Time to correct that. Looking successful and acting confident went a long way toward becoming successful. Or so her mother had always taught her. To that end, she donned a new pair of brown slacks and a pale gold shirt and secured a thick gold link bracelet around her right wrist.

Then she rounded up the dogs, using more treats to lure them out into their run alongside the house.

Cat finally headed for the kitchen, reminiscent

of the fifties when it had been last renovated, other than the appliances that had been replaced several years ago. Even if she had a barrel-load of extra cash, she wouldn't update the kitchen more than necessary. She'd been serious when she'd warned Aidan about her cooking skills—they were at a bare minimum. She spent as much time outside with the horses as she could manage.

She'd barely set the table when she heard the back door open.

"Aidan?"

"Aye."

The in-law apartment had its own separate entry out back. She turned to see him come into the kitchen, his shoulders nearly filling the doorway. As had happened the first time she'd met him, he took away her breath for a moment. It wasn't simply that he was attractive—which he was—but that he had a way about him that narrowed her focus so she couldn't see anything beyond him. He'd changed into a fresh shirt, and his thick hair looked damp, as if he'd slicked it back with wet hands. Feeling herself flush, Cat blinked and turned toward the counter with the Crock-Pot.

"I just have to put the food on the table." She removed the cover.

"'Tis making my mouth water already," he said,

moving close enough behind her that she nearly dropped the meat fork. "What can I do to help?"

"Sit." Cat waited until he moved away from her to set the meat on a platter. "Everything's ready," she said, adding potatoes and carrots and then ladling thickened beef broth over everything.

"Looks perfect."

"I hope you're not disappointed." Carrying the platter to the table set in a nook surrounded by big windows with a view of the pastures, she put it down between the two place settings. "I'm not much of a cook."

"I think you're anything you set your mind to be."

"What makes you so sure?"

"A young lass running a grand business this size is pretty impressive."

Charmed by the very Irishness of his wording in addition to the lilt, Cat sat opposite him and indicated he should help himself. "I didn't start the business, but I've worked with the horses since I was a teenager."

"So it was a family operation, then?"

"Right. Both Mom and Dad ran it ever since I can remember. I always wanted to help them, but they made me wait until I was thirteen. They even paid me a salary. Which of course they made me save to pay for college rather than spend."

After heaping his plate with food, Aidan passed the platter to her. "No sisters or brothers?"

"One brother. Jens liked riding horses well enough, but he hated the work involved in taking care of them. Particularly having to help with the breeding—rather the cleanup after—even more. He would disappear whenever possible. So he graduated from the Kellogg MBA program and then took a job as far away from here as he could get. New York City."

"'Tis a shame. That he hated the work, I mean. I understand the other part. Sometimes you do need to get away from family."

Why had Aidan needed to get away from his brother? Cat wondered as she filled her plate.

Remembering the argument she'd witnessed, she thought it was likely that they didn't agree on how to run their business. Good, then, that he was a trainer and she was a breeder. Hopefully there'd be no reason for either of them to step on the other's toes. A perfect partnership. The phone call she'd gotten at the time, about George being missing and about Jack moving up the court date, had put her in a foul mood, an impression she was eager to correct.

Cat wanted to believe they had a fresh start and that she'd been worried for nothing.

Aidan dug into the food. "Your parents can't be very old, Cat. Why did they leave the farm?"

She sighed. "As much as I love the business, I wish they were still here. Everything seemed perfect, like good fortune would go on forever, until the economy tanked. The stress got to Dad in a big way and he had a heart attack, thankfully not fatal. It was enough for Mom, though. She made him retire early."

Mom had feared Dad would just drop dead someday. The idea had scared Cat, too.

"So they sold you the farm?"

"The land itself is in a family trust, but they gave me the business and I give them a percentage of the profit to make their retirement easier." Another reason she wanted to restore her financial footing. "Like I said, Jens didn't want anything to do with it, so he was glad that I took it over. It would have devastated Dad if the business didn't stay in the family. That was nearly three years ago."

Just before she'd gotten involved with Jack.

Cat took a big bite of pot roast and remembered how lonely and trusting she'd been. Unfortunately she'd trusted the wrong man. A rookie horse trainer, Jack had put on a good show as to how he was all about her work and how he was willing to help her run the farm, but it had all been lies. The pretense hadn't lasted long once they were married. Within six months, she'd started to suspect that he was more interested in the money the business could make for him than he was in her. She'd done everything to make it not so, but as Dad used to say, you couldn't change a leopard's spots. Still, it wasn't until she'd learned about Simone that Cat had kicked him out.

Swallowing the food that had suddenly gone tasteless, she said, "Anyway, my parents moved to Arkansas because Mom feared that if they stayed in the area, *retirement* would only be a word."

"Arkansas is one of your states, is it not?"

"Right. It might as well be another country for as often as I get to see them." Realizing Aidan had no idea of the huge distances one could travel in this country compared to his own, she explained, "It would be like you going from Dublin to Paris to see your family."

"That would be quite a distance, indeed. You must miss them, then."

"All the time. They come for a couple of weeks in the summer and at Christmas. I try to get to Arkansas for a visit in between, but I can't leave the place for too long. And days or even weeks just isn't enough when you're used to seeing someone every day of your life. I take it you don't feel the same way about Cashel."

Aidan laughed. "No, I am not missing him, not yet. I think we needed what you call a time out. 'Tis my younger brother Tiernan I miss. He lives here in America, and I have not seen him for nearly two years."

"He's training horses?"

Aidan's smile softened the hard planes of his face. "Aye, but not Thoroughbreds. Your Western horses. He has a small horse ranch in a place called South Dakota. Would that be as far as Arkansas?"

"Oh, much farther. Nearly twice as far."

The smile faded a bit. "Nevertheless, I'm hoping I'll see him and meet his wife, Ella, sometime this summer." He forked the last bite of meat from his plate and said, "By the way, the pot roast is excellent."

"Thanks." She indicated the platter that still held half the pot roast. "Help yourself."

"I don't mind if I do." Aidan took seconds.

Cat said, "Eat all you want, no rush. When I'm done, I need to get over to the barn to check on the mare I bred this morning."

"If you would not mind waiting a few minutes, I would go with you to check on Mac Finnian."

"Yes, of course."

He ate in silence for a moment, his expression pensive. Then he said, "When I was in the barn earlier, I saw no other workers. Surely Raul is not your only employee."

A statement that reminded Cat of one of the reasons she was so desperate to take a chance on Mac. "Bernie Hansen is full-time now," she said, feeling her stomach tighten. "Bernie was off picking up supplies when you came in. And then there's Vincent and Laura. They come after school every day they can."

"So you only have two full-time employees and two children."

On the defensive now, she argued, "Those 'children' are teenagers, and they work hard mucking out stalls, hauling bales of hay, grooming horses."

"But surely that is not enough to run a breeding farm this size when the operation is in full swing."

"Then I'll hire another couple men when business picks up."

"What about a barn manager?"

"I'm doing double duty for the time being. I had a barn manager until recently."

"You said something about that in Galway. That was weeks ago. Surely you have thought of replacing him."

She shook her head. "I keep hoping he'll show up."

"What happened?"

"I really don't know. No one seems to. George worked for my parents," Cat said stiffly, starting to feel like Aidan was backing her into a corner. "I never remember a time when he wasn't here. He left while I was in Ireland and I'm hoping he'll come back."

"If he quit his job, why do you think he might show up again."

"That's the thing. He didn't quit." Once again, an awful feeling engulfed her. "He simply disappeared. No one knows where he went."

When Aidan fell silent, Cat bristled.

Was he silently blaming her?

Or silently criticizing her for not replacing George?

And for not adding more workers?

She couldn't afford to hire anyone else right now, not even a new barn manager. If George came back, she would find a way to pay him again. She hadn't given up on him yet, even though she couldn't stop worrying that something had happened to make him leave.

That his disappearance was somehow her fault.

## *Chapter Four*

"I cannot eat another bite. Allow me to help clear," Aidan said, rising and taking the platter and his plate to the counter.

"Thanks," Cat muttered, head ducked away from him as she scooped up the flatware and threw it on her plate.

He wondered what he and Cashel had gotten themselves into. Bad enough his partner had attitude and an angry ex-husband, but now to learn Cat didn't have enough help made him worry that she didn't have the finances to carry out their contract.

Had he left Ireland simply to waste his time?

The entry fee into a graded stakes race was thousands of American dollars. And what about the six-figure entry fee to the Breeders' Cup Classic? The hope was that Mac could earn the money through the wins that would qualify him for the world-class meet, or, better yet, that he would win a Breeders' Cup Challenge race. Aidan was confident that given decent weather conditions and no injuries, Mac could outrun his competition on any dirt track.

But what if the payoff wasn't enough?

What if he didn't win a Challenge?

Could Cat really come up with six figures when she apparently couldn't afford to hire more workers?

Not wanting to get into it now lest he say something that he would regret, Aidan tabled that particular discussion for later. On edge, his gut in a knot, he forced himself to relax. Cat didn't seem to be having an easy time of it, either.

They remained silent as they finished clearing.

When the last item was in the dishwasher, the leftovers in the refrigerator, she asked, "Ready to take that walk over to the barn?"

"And eager. I want to make sure Mac has settled in."

Aidan followed Cat out the door and then walked beside her. As if the very action of taking one step after another was medicinal, he felt his inner tension dissolve. A quick glance Cat's way told him she was more at ease, as well. He had no criticism of the grounds nor the barn, so, enough help or no, she was somehow managing to do things right. He had to give her the benefit of the doubt.

"Dean's truck," she murmured, and Aidan followed her gaze to the dark blue truck parked to one side of the barn.

Also noting the old silver sedan parked opposite the truck, he asked, "A couple of your clients?"

"My high school workers are here. And one of my two big clients at the moment. A few weeks ago, Dean Hill decided to change barns, and he wanted me to be in charge of breeding his mares. As a matter of fact, I bred one of his mares this morning. No doubt he's here to check on her, as well."

"How many mares does he own?"

"He brought eleven here. But they're not being bred to Dangerous Illusion. That's my stallion. He's a little high-strung and low on the champion totem pole. Dean brought his own stallion. You might have heard of him—False Promise."

"I know the name."

"You should. Last year he won three consecutive graded stakes races, was third in the Kentucky Derby and won the Preakness."

"I remember…didn't he have a twin who raced, as well?"

"Right, but unfortunately, Memory of You broke down as a two-year-old, so his career ended and he never had the chance to make a name for himself. False Promise was headed for the Breeders' Cup Classic and probably Horse of the Year, but a fracture to his rear right leg just before the Belmont Stakes ended his racing career, too."

Having experienced one of the horses he'd trained breaking down himself, Aidan could imagine the owner's despair at such a horrible turn of fate. "Thankfully the horse survived. And the jockey." At least the accident wasn't the tragedy that Aidan knew it could have been.

"Yes, both survived and the horse healed well," Cat said, as they entered the barn. "His racing career might be over, but at least he can stand at stud and possibly sire future champions."

A consolation, Aidan thought, one that could never make up for the loss of a dream. Most owners didn't get more than a single chance at a really fine colt or filly that could win the high stakes races. Winning was the dream of every owner and trainer and jockey, of every groom and hotwalker who came into contact with a fine piece of horseflesh. A whole team of support staff considered the horse their own.

He assumed the dream would be the same for the breeder. Isn't that why Cat made the deal with them? She wanted Mac to cover her broodmares and perhaps give her the next generation of winners. He'd felt that spark burn in her at their first meeting.

Would she sell the foals? he wondered. Or did

she have dreams of racing them herself? Not unheard of if she had the finances to do so.

Cat stopped in the aisle. "I'm going this way." She indicated a direction away from Mac's box stall. "Would you like to meet Dean? You never know when he might be looking for a new trainer or know another owner who's looking to hire someone."

"Aye, thank you."

Another way to make some necessary money, Aidan thought. Kind of Cat to help him outside of their contract. He'd come to America not knowing what to expect from her, and while she did seem too much on edge, he suspected she had good reason. He thought she really was a caring sort, as he'd heard when she'd spoken of her missing barn manager. He needed to revise his thinking a bit, not be so uptight around her. Her intentions were good, and she'd gotten Mac and him here. He had to trust she had the financial assets to carry through. Perhaps that was why she hesitated hiring more help. A matter of budget.

Perhaps if he relaxed, he could more easily control what the dream had foretold.

He followed Cat down a side aisle and toward the back, where a silver-haired man—Dean Hill, he assumed—was deep in conversation with Raul. Both men appeared intense, as if they were arguing about something.

Was there a problem with the mare?

Then the client looked up to see them coming and dismissed Raul, who quickly headed for the back of the barn.

"Ah, Cat, there you are," Hill said. "I just came to check on Fairy Tail."

"She has seemed fine all day."

"She looks good, and Raul said her appetite is normal," Dean said, his dark gaze zeroing in on Aidan. "New client?"

"New partner, new venture," Cat said. "Dean, this is Aidan McKenna, one of Ireland's best trainers."

Aidan started at the unexpected compliment and held out a hand to Hill. The man was younger than his silver hair indicated, perhaps in his early forties. His narrow face was smooth but for a few crinkles at the outside corner of his brown eyes.

Dean looked him up and down before taking the offered hand. "McKenna…that's familiar."

Aidan noted the other man's fierce grip as they shook. His was trim but muscular. "My brother Cashel and I are trainers. We own McKenna Racing. A few years back, we had a horse place in the Arlington Million." And with their share of the winnings, they'd had enough money to buy an exceptional filly they had trained from the owners they worked for. Plus they'd been able to pay an exorbitant stud fee to get Mac.

"So you're what?" Hill asked. "Expanding to the U.S.?"

"Something like that, at least for the racing season."

"And at least one breeding season," Cat added. "That's where I come into the partnership." She stepped back. "Excuse me while I look in on Fairy Tail."

"Good, good," Dean said without taking his eyes off Aidan.

Odd that the man didn't follow Cat into the stall, Aidan thought. When Mac's dam, Bold Lass, was being bred, he'd wanted to know every detail of everything that was going on. Then again, the owner did have eleven mares. Perhaps he'd had too much experience to want to know every detail.

"So what are your immediate plans?" Hill asked.

"To run my colt in some upcoming graded stakes races."

"Your colt. You mean you train him."

"And own him, as well. My brother Cashel and I bought his dam and bred her."

"So you're expanding the business," Hill said.

"In this one case. I'm a trainer at heart," Aidan admitted. "I'm more interested in training colts and fillies to win than in producing foals."

"Why bring him here to run him on dirt?"

"That's the grand challenge. Mac Finnian is faster on dirt than he is on grass."

Hill's eyebrows shot up. "Well, well, he'll probably be running against one of my colts eventually. I have a training farm just down the road, and I have a couple of colts who are ready for the right race. I'll have to keep an eye on you."

Before Aidan could question him about which colt, which race, Cat left the broodmare's stall saying, "Fairy Tail looks good."

Hill gave her a once-over, as if meeting her for the first time. "As do you, dear Cat. I don't believe I've ever seen you in such elegant splendor."

Cat laughed. "What? Muck-covered jeans and sweatshirts aren't elegant?"

"You're a natural beauty, no matter what you wear."

Aidan listened to the interchange in silence. Considering how charming Hill was being, he must be taken with Cat. Aidan didn't blame him. The fine-looking lass had invaded his dreams, after all. "Glad to meet you, Hill. I need to see to my colt now."

"And I need to get going. I have some business to take care of myself." The man focused back on Cat. "I'm confident that together, we're going to produce a spectacular crop of foals next spring."

"That's the plan."

"Two down and nine to go." Hill indicated Fairy Tail. "Or perhaps it's three and eight."

Aidan started to move off.

"Hopefully. And hopefully the first foal born will be a champion," Cat said, then called, "Aidan, wait up." She rushed to catch up to him. "I would like to check on Mac myself."

There was a touch of possessiveness in her tone that made Aidan clench his jaw. He told himself that she simply wanted to see to the colt's welfare now that he was in her barn, and he couldn't fault her for that.

Horses along the aisle hung out their heads as they passed. Aidan patted every one on his side and noted that Cat did the same on the other. Her love for horses was evident in her gentle touch and in the soft murmurings with which she greeted each mare. All twelve box stalls in the aisle were in use.

"So all of these are Hill's mares, and two of them already pregnant."

"That kind of surprised me, too, that both got pregnant in their first season. We'll see about Fairy Tail. Another of Dean's mares is about to ovulate, as well. The vet'll palpate her tomorrow to see if she's ready to meet False Promise."

"This lad?" he asked, when they reached the end of the aisle where a blood bay stallion with a white star on his forehead dozed in his stall.

Aidan stopped at the door to take a better look.

Cat stopped next to him, too close for his comfort. Her arm brushing his left a swath of heat shooting through him.

"That's Dean's champion," she confirmed.

"Aye, he's a handsome lad. He should sire some grand foals."

"Fingers crossed. I have other clients, too. They share the aisle on the other side of the barn. Right now, only eight of the stalls are in use. Martin Bradley brought in four of his broodmares and his own stallion from his farm," she said, mindful of Jack's threat to bring in the horses she used to own, as well. "My own horses—six mares, a stallion, a teaser and two geldings—are in the middle aisle. Plus Mac," she added.

Again she spoke in a possessive tone, as if the colt belonged to her. Aidan fought a twitch of discomfort.

"Mac won't be there for long," he assured her. "The first stakes race is barely two weeks away. We need to get him in a stall at the track so he can start working out there every morning and so I can find a jockey. Unless you've already made all the arrangements."

"No, of course not. I got the paperwork going, and I planned to take you over there tomorrow, so you can see the facility and the stalls available. How would I know your preference?"

Aidan told himself to relax already. He didn't need to go looking for trouble. No matter that he'd feared he'd gone from the frying pan into the fire, Cat wasn't his older brother. She wasn't making decisions for him as Cashel would.

"In the meantime, I have a short track opposite the pastures." She moved away from the stallion. "You can start stretching Mac's legs tomorrow before we go to the track if you want."

"That sounds like a fine idea, though he won't be breaking any speed records with me on his back."

"Just think of how much faster he'll be when he gets a lightweight jockey."

A few seconds later, Aidan heard a man's deep voice call out, "Cat, you in here?"

"Over here, Martin," she called, then lowered her voice. "My other best client."

A burly man with unnaturally dark hair, as if it had been dyed, popped out of the far aisle. "We brought Sweetpea Sue a little early."

"We?"

He stepped his aviator glasses up the bridge of his nose. "Simone is putting her in the stall next to Quick Pick."

Cat forced a smile. "No problem."

"The problem is Quick Pick isn't pregnant yet."

"Quick Pick was a maiden. You need to be patient, Martin. We'll try again as soon as she goes back in season."

A maiden not conceiving in her first season wasn't unexpected, but Aidan picked up on the strain in Cat's voice. Was there some reason for her to be nervous?

Dressed as if she were about to go riding, a lovely blonde stepped next to her father. "What about Abigail Runs? Why isn't she pregnant?"

Cat sounded like she was about to choke when she turned to her client. "Martin, are you unhappy about something? You've been with me for three years. You know I always do the very best for you."

"Hill already has two pregnant mares and this is his first breeding season with you."

"Sheer luck. You're not in a competition. Not here, away from the track. Just give it some time."

The man grunted and gave Aidan a once-over. "You the Irishman Jack told me about?"

"That I would be," Aidan agreed, holding out his hand. "Aidan McKenna."

"Martin Bradley," the other man said, taking Aidan's hand and shaking. "My daughter, Simone."

Aidan noted how Cat's jaw clenched.

He nodded at the blonde. "Miss Bradley."

Simone held out her hand, and when Aidan took it, she gave Cat a smug smile. "A pleasure."

Aidan sensed Cat's immediate *dis*pleasure.

She asked, "Martin, are you thinking of bringing in more than the mares we originally discussed?"

"Where would you get that idea?"

"Just checking so I can hold open more spots if needed."

Aidan thought she sounded relieved.

"Gotta get going," Martin said, whirling back the way he came. "C'mon, Simone."

The daughter gave Aidan one last look before following.

Cat called after him. "I'll let you know when one of your mares comes into season."

Aidan felt the tension drain out of her.

"Do you and Martin not get along?"

"We get along just fine," she said in a clipped tone that didn't convince him. Could be the problem wasn't the man but his daughter.

Suddenly a screech filled the air. Aidan started but Cat seemed to loosen up immediately.

"No need to worry," she assured him. "Teenagers are rarely quiet."

As they rounded the empty box stall at the aisle's end, he could hear a girl's indignant voice. "You think you're so funny, I wonder how you'd look with a shovelful of horse manure on your head!"

"Let's not try it to find out!" Cat said, her order followed by silence.

They turned into the center aisle where Mac Finnian was stabled. Two teenagers—a thin blonde and a husky, dark-haired boy—were squared off. Aidan realized they must be Laura and Vincent, Cat's part-time workers. Her face flushed, Laura was brushing off her derriere while Vincent tried to hide a grin.

"Are you working or playing?" Cat asked.

"Working," they said in unison.

"Get to it, then."

Laura gave Vincent a shove before grabbing a mucking rake and disappearing into a box stall. Vincent snorted and did the same on the other side of the aisle.

Cat moved in close and whispered, "Vincent has a crush on Laura. What he doesn't realize yet is that she has a crush on him, too."

When her breast brushed against his arm, Aidan sucked in a quick breath. "'Tis a wonder they get any work done."

Cat's good will disappeared in a snap and she stepped back. Aidan couldn't read humans in the same way he could horses, but he wasn't dense. She'd clearly taken that as a criticism. She certainly was on edge with him. He was glad when they got to Mac's stall, but for once, the colt didn't stick out his head to greet him. Instead, he paced the small space in a tight circle.

Immediately concerned, Aidan murmured, "Mac, what's up with you, lad?"

The colt stopped short of the door, so Aidan opened it and stepped in, too aware of Cat right behind him. He reached out for the colt, ran a hand up Mac's cheek to his forehead and then scratched his poll.

"Is he all right?"

"He's nervous, but after what he's been through the last couple of weeks, that should come as no surprise."

Except that it did. Mac was normally settled, unaffected by change or surprises. But there was something about this place that got to him. That made his flesh quiver when touched. Aidan had noticed it earlier when he'd brought the colt inside the barn. Then, too, he'd put the colt's unease to the strain of the long move.

Unfortunately, Mac still hadn't settled down.

Aidan could sense the colt's stress as he moved closer and continued to stroke him. No matter that he ran his hands over Mac's neck and back and chest, Aidan couldn't read him, couldn't say why Mac had gotten so rattled. Frowning, he took a peppermint from his pocket, and offered it to the colt. For a moment, he didn't think Mac would take the candy. His gut tightened. Was Mac sick?

Then the colt moved closer and brushed Aidan's palm with his muzzle and lipped the peppermint before gently taking it with his teeth.

A sense of relief washed through Aidan until Cat said, "I think I should call Helen. That's the vet—Helen Fox."

"He doesn't need a vet. He's not ill."

"I can see how concerned you are, Aidan. We can't let anything happen to him—"

"I shall decide if and when he needs a veterinarian."

They stared at each other for a moment. The silence was deafening.

"I know he's your colt, Aidan, but I have a big investment in his well-being. And this is my barn. I'm responsible—"

"I know that. And I know you want what's best for any horse in your care, Cat, but I know Mac. He simply is stressed by the move, is all. I feel him relaxing already."

Which was true. Horseflesh softened under his touch as he continued to stroke the colt. Mac undoubtedly needed a bit of reassurance, was all. Considering his deep connection to Mac, Aidan would surely know if there was something more about which to be alarmed.

Cat nodded. "Fine. I didn't mean to question your judgment. I was simply concerned."

"We'll both keep an eye on him tonight, then,"

Aidan said, trying to defuse the tension now between them. "Just to be certain."

"All right. When I check on Fairy Tail, I'll check on Mac, as well."

"I would appreciate that. As well as you telling me if you find anything off about the lad."

All this walking on eggshells was starting to get to Aidan, but he felt like he couldn't be himself, couldn't feel free to say what he wanted.

Cat obviously loved horses as much as he—they had that in common. He quickly quashed the rush of longing that shot through him. He'd almost forgotten what it felt like to have any kind of relationship with an attractive lass in the very industry that took up every moment of his life. There was something exciting about sharing work as well as play with the same woman. Not that he and Cat had a personal relationship or ever would.

Pegeen's tragic death nine months before broke his heart, and he wasn't going to replace her.

No one ever could.

*SHE TOOK HIS SWOLLEN tip in her mouth, drew him deeper and then into her throat, inch by inch. Her nails scraped the insides of his thighs and he thought he would pop like a champagne cork, but she stopped just in time. She knew exactly what to do with him, how to make him insane with desire.*

*Each time they were together, he learned she had new tricks.*

*He closed his eyes and let her work him and just as he was about to find release...*

An inhuman scream woke him.

## *Chapter Five*

A sound…a scream more than a whinny…woke Cat.

She bolted upright in bed and listened for a repeat. The night was silent but for the wind whistling around the house. A storm was imminent but the skies hadn't yet opened.

The dogs were relaxed, curled up on their beds, their heads raised so they could watch her.

Taking a deep breath, Cat willed her rapidly pounding heart to still. She must have been dreaming. She checked her bedside clock. Three in the morning.

Awake now, she decided to get up and check on Fairy Tail. And Mac. She might as well do it now, before the rain started and made things uncomfortable. Wearing only a thin nightgown, she pulled on the jeans she'd thrown over a chair.

Sleep had eluded her for hours. She'd been restless and out of sorts all evening. Aware of Aidan in the in-law apartment below her, she kept imagining him arguing with her, giving her looks that sent shivers down her spine.

Not shivers of fear.

Just the opposite.

What the heck was wrong with her? she wondered.

Something about him tugged at her. It wasn't just his looks or his obvious sexuality. Something that came from inside. The deep love he had for the horses he trained had been so obvious when he'd checked on Mac earlier. It was an emotion she understood. One Jack had never had. Too bad she hadn't realized that when she'd met him.

She pulled on her boots.

Expressions hopeful, Smokey and Topaz left their beds.

"All right, you know you can go out anytime you need to." They had a doggy door to the run, but apparently they were after more than a brief outing. She patted them both as she got to her feet. "Sorry, no walks in the middle of the night."

Looking at her empty bed, she knew exactly what was wrong with her. She hadn't gotten as lucky as one of the broodmares in her barn for nearly a year. The moment she'd discovered Jack's infidelity, she'd kicked him out of her bed, and no man had replaced him. Yet. Every time she bred one of the mares, she wondered when it would be her turn to feel a man over her and inside her.

Only, not Jack.

She hadn't been able to imagine with whom until now.

Aidan's chiseled features suddenly filled her mind. This would never do. She had to get the Irishman out of her thoughts. She couldn't have fantasies of her business partner or she would never be able to work with him.

Leaving her bedroom, dogs at her heels, Cat walked through the dark house to the back door.

"Your run is that way." She pointed and the dogs reluctantly headed for the doggie door.

Her eyes adjusted quickly once outside, the dusk-to-dawn light on the exterior of the barn was her only illumination now. The moon remained hidden by storm clouds. A gust of wind tore at her nightshirt so that it billowed around her like a sail. The air that sneaked under the material was chilly and humid, heavy with unshed rain. She gladly escaped it as she ran into the barn.

Leaving lights on all night would mess with the normal reproductive patterns of the mares, so the barn was dark.

Since she was only checking on Fairy Tail and Mac, and not wanting to disturb the others who should be sleeping, she took one of the combination flashlight/lanterns from a hook near the door and used it to guide her to the aisle housing the Hill mares. Whenever she entered the barn at night after a mare was covered, Cat always tried to be as quiet and unobtrusive as possible so as not to awaken more of the horses than she needed to.

But tonight, a low nicker from one side of the barn and the sound of hooves clicking against the stall boards on the other made her stop short. She listened intently, but heard nothing that should disturb the horses.

So why were they awake?

She could hear sounds in every direction as horses moved around their stalls. At three o'clock in the morning. Daylight was still two hours away.

What had happened to agitate them?

For a moment, Cat had the distinct feeling she wasn't alone, that someone else was in the barn with her.

At three in the morning!

Heart drumming in her ears, she listened past the thrum of her own pulse speeding up, searched for another presence.

Was that a footstep she heard? A human breath?

"Is someone in here?" she called out.

No answer.

"Raul?" Her mouth went dry. She held her breath and concentrated on picking up the slightest sound. "Bernie?"

A little freaked, she told herself she was imagining things. No one else was anywhere around.

No human anyway. The horses quieted down, a single nicker from across the barn the only sound of disturbance.

With no other apparent reason, Cat put their restless behavior to the coming storm. Wind unsettled horses and made them more likely to spook at any little rustle, because pinpointing the source was nearly impossible. Horses were flight rather than fight animals. Any strange sound could mean a predator approaching, which would kick up their nerves.

Just then the wind whistled into the barn and up the aisle and the restlessness around her increased once more.

The coming storm. That had to be it.

Relaxing, she took a deep breath and moved down the aisle, stopping only when she reached Fairy Tail's stall. She switched her flashlight to lantern mode so that it would give the area a soft glow and not bother the horse's eyes.

Seeing that the mare stood away from the door, Cat wondered why she didn't step forward as she usually did. Fairy Tail normally loved the attention Cat gave her.

"Hey, girl, how are you doing?" Cat called softly.

The mare backed up into the farthest corner, pulled her head high and snorted. Cat could see the mare's dark eyes staring at her. That and the snort translated into the mare worrying about some hidden danger.

"It's me, sweetheart. I'm not going to hurt you."

Cat clipped the lantern to a jeans loop and freed her hands, and as she slowly moved forward, held out one of her hands in a nonthreatening way. The mare was so spooked by the wind that she didn't trust her. Cat kept talking nonsense in a soft voice, anything to soothe the mare. Her being so stressed wasn't good, and Cat feared that it would interfere with her conceiving.

"Relax, girl, that's it," Cat murmured as the mare finally lowered her head and stretched out her neck so Cat could touch her. "Yes, you know me. You know there's no reason to be afraid."

But as she ran a hand along the mare's neck, her horseflesh quivered. Fairy Tail was afraid of something. And the wind wasn't even whipping through the barn now.

Had Fairy Tail been hurt by the stallion's cover that morning?

Had she missed something in checking over the mare?

Continuing her soothing chatter, Cat rechecked every inch of the mare's body for scratches or bites she might have gotten from False Promise, but she found nothing. Fairy Tail was physically fine as far as she could see. And given Cat's continued attention, she finally settled. So the mare wasn't hurt, just frightened.

"You are a scaredy mare," Cat whispered, kissing the velvety soft nose. A rush of warm breath on her cheek in return made her smile and pat the mare's neck. "Are you going to be okay now if I leave you?"

Fairy Tail pushed at her in response, making Cat laugh.

"That's my girl."

Relieved, she left the stall and got that weird feeling of not being alone again. But though she stopped and waited and listened for something that would indicate another human presence, nothing seemed out of place. It was more an itchy feeling of something being wrong.

Not wanting to stay in the barn any longer than necessary, Cat headed for the center aisle and Mac Finnian's stall. The colt was acting nearly as weird as Fairy Tail. But like the mare, he quickly settled under her soothing hands. Other than the tension that rippled through the barn, he seemed just fine.

A rumble of thunder followed by a flash of light through the open doors set off the horses once more. They began to shift and nicker.

What a night—she'd never seen them all so edgy.

She'd never felt so edgy being in the barn alone.

It was almost as if something horrible was about to happen here.

Then the tap-tap of rain hitting the roof made Cat groan. The storm had started in earnest.

Deciding to get to the house before the sky opened and the drizzle turned into a downpour, she left the flashlight on its hook and made a run for it. The rain beat down on her harder than she expected. She tucked her chin to her chest and ran blindly toward the house.

The wet ground beneath her feet made going treacherous, and halfway there, she slipped, slid and caught herself only to ram into another body. Arms wrapped tight around her.

Instinct made her fight and start to scream until a hand whipped over her mouth to hush her.

CERTAIN THAT SHE'D LEFT THE BARN, he left the shadows where he'd been hiding. She'd passed right by him without even knowing he was there.

What the hell had she been doing out here anyway?

Five minutes earlier and she would have caught them. She could still catch them. They weren't by any means done with their work.

He considered the risk.

Considered the reward.

Considered what would have to be done if one night Cat entered the barn at the wrong time.

He decided he couldn't let it matter—the risk was worth whatever they had to do.

They'd gotten rid of one obstacle.

Cat was equally disposable.

## *Chapter Six*

Cat bit down on the hand covering her mouth—hard!—until he let her go.

"What the—"

"Aidan?"

His name came out a screech that attacked his ears.

"Aye," he growled in return.

"What do you think you're doing?"

"Trying to be a gentleman, is all. If I hadn't caught you, you would be butt-down in the mud now."

She gaped at him as if trying to come up with some stinging retort.

The rain was coming down harder. Aidan had no patience for her temper, especially since she'd felt so good up against him. The dream hovered in his mind…he'd had no release and he was fighting to ignore his continued arousal. He pressed a hand against her arm to get her moving toward the house again.

A moment later, they were inside, dripping water and leaving blobs of mud in their path along the kitchen floor.

"How long were you out there?" she demanded to know. "Were you in the barn when I called out?"

His gut tightened. "Someone was in the barn?"

"I thought so…but probably not. The storm had the horses worked up. My imagination, too."

Staring at her worked up *his* imagination. Brought to mind the dreams he'd had of her. She looked like a beautiful water sprite, wet ringlets around her face, the filmy thing she wore soaking wet and clinging to her breasts, outlining nipples that begged for his personal attention.

If his dreams were truthful, he knew exactly what she liked.

"See something you like?" she asked.

Aidan jerked up his head, but there was nothing he could do about his lower parts. She was staring at him wide-eyed. He could see a fast pulse beating in her throat. Her mind was on the same track as his. Raw desire cut through him. He waited for her to say something, to dispel the heat that was building in him to a point of discomfort.

He fought his instincts, fought the dreams. Still…

Unable to help himself, he stepped closer, just to test her. So close that her breasts, now mere centimeters from his chest, seemed to strain against the thin cloth to reach out and touch him.

He said, "I heard you go out to the barn quite a while ago."

He lifted a strand of her wet hair and curled it around his finger. Waited for her to move. To say something. She did neither.

"I waited for you to return, Cat."

He could hear her breath. Uneven. Her trying to control it. Him trying to control himself in response.

"But you didn't."

Still she didn't say anything. Stared into his eyes. Licked her lips and left them parted. Tempting him. On purpose? Could he really resist?

"You were gone so long I thought something was wrong. I was a bit worried, thought I ought to check on you, to make sure you were safe."

He had her backed up against the sink now, his erection lightly brushing the V at her upper thighs. Sliding his hands around her hips, he pulled her against him so that she could feel his need.

And then she kissed him.

Her mouth opened to him, invited him, greedily took his tongue. The kiss was deep and hard and hot. He slid his hands up to her breasts, plucked the turgid nipples through the thin material. She moaned into his mouth. And she began to move against him, Pressing. Rocking. Bringing him nearly to the brink fully clothed.

He imagined her taking him in her mouth… opening her thighs…letting him do anything and everything to her…

A crack of thunder startled him into ending the kiss.

Lightning lit the room. Lit her. Wanton features. Ripe breasts barely hidden by fabric that made them even more tempting.

He'd been ready to take her right there, to rip off her clothes, heft her onto the sink and take her.

*The dreams...*

He remembered his vow.

Getting a grip on himself, he stepped back. What in the world had he been thinking?

Well, that was the problem, then—he hadn't been thinking at all.

He had to get hold of himself, not let nature's instincts lead him into making another huge mistake.

He had to say something to make things right.

Seeing her face, he let his apology freeze on his tongue.

No anger there. No regret. Her expression told him she was intrigued.

And yet she was able to pull away, saying, "I'm going back to bed now."

In the doorway, she looked over her shoulder

once, as if to see what he would do about that. When he didn't follow, she left the kitchen.

Wanting in the worst way to follow, to take her up on her unasked invitation, he watched her go with great regret.

When he was able to walk again, he took himself back downstairs.

The in-law apartment was two rooms and a bath. He walked through the living area with its upholstered sofa and chair, a small galley kitchen and a table, and into the bedroom. Throwing himself in bed, he waited for sleep…and the dream…to reclaim him.

THE DOGS' BARKING *confused him.*

*Where was she?*

*They weren't friendly barks. Nor barks of warning.*

*Something pitiful vibrated through their voices and one of them began to howl. The other was digging desperately, and his stomach knotted as he waited to see what was buried beneath the earth….*

Only, his eyes flashed open too soon.

A nightmare.

His heart pounded, and blood coursed through him.

He'd gone to bed expecting to be sexually satisfied, at least in his dream, and instead a nightmare left a taste of dread that kept him awake the rest of the night.

It all seemed unreal to Cat when she woke at daybreak. Though he hadn't followed her into her bed and she'd had to take care of the potential frustration herself, she'd dreamed of Aidan. Of everything he could do to her and she could do to him. Just thinking about it now made her edgy. The bed was too empty, so she left it and jumped in the shower.

One thing she wasn't was shy about sex. How could she be, considering her profession? She'd had a mind-bending sex life with Jack…well, until she hadn't. He'd had her believing so many lies that once she learned the truth anything between them sexual or otherwise had been over. A year of celibacy was enough. She was open to having another man in her bed.

She decided there was no need to be embarrassed because Aidan had changed his mind. Undoubtedly, he'd simply thought twice about the implications of their sleeping together while working together.

Then again, perhaps he'd remembered she was the person in the partnership who had the money.

Even if it wasn't literally true, even if she'd had to borrow the money to bring Mac Finnian from Ireland, the thought hit too close to home, reminded her of her relationship with Jack. When she'd met her ex-husband, he'd been charming and sexy and broke. She'd been susceptible both emotionally and physically and therefore had made the biggest mistake of her life. She didn't need another situation like that with a man, so perhaps things had turned out for the best.

After a quick breakfast, Cat fed the dogs and took them out with her when she left the house. They wanted to follow her into the barn, which was fine with her horses, but she wasn't certain about Hill's or the other four.

"No." She pointed to an empty pasture. "Over there. Go!"

Topaz looked doubtful, but when Smokey took off, she followed. The dogs had roaming privileges on her property; an electric fence kept them from straying elsewhere.

Cat entered the barn. Raul and Bernie were already inside, mucking out stalls. After checking to make sure Fairy Tail had gotten over whatever had been freaking her out in the middle of the night, Cat made for Mac's stall. To her surprise, it was empty.

"McKenna took his colt outside to work him."

She turned around to find Bernie behind her. "Thanks. I was a little surprised. He certainly got out here early enough."

"He was already checking over the colt when I came in. That horse looks like a powerhouse to me. Great investment."

"From your lips, Bernie." Everything counted

on her being right about Mac. "We could use an infusion of money. Hopefully I'll be able to give you and Raul a raise before summer is out."

"I know I'd appreciate one."

In his early twenties, Bernie Hansen was tall and broad and strong as an ox, which made him perfect for this work despite his college degree. Still she couldn't help but be curious as to why he hadn't gotten a job in his field. Tricked out in a suit and tie, he was more than presentable with a neat haircut and a smile that crinkled the corners of his brown eyes.

Maybe there simply weren't any available jobs and he took this one because it was familiar work—he'd been raised on a farm. He hadn't quite worked for her long enough for her to be comfortable probing into his personal life.

Thinking about her middle-of-the-night scare, Cat asked, "Bernie, were you in the barn last night?"

He started. "Me? When?"

Caught by the tension he suddenly exuded, Cat frowned. She'd simply hoped he would put her mind at ease. "About three in the morning."

"Nope, not me, Miss Clarke. I was in bed by eleven. I need my beauty rest," he joked.

Either he'd relaxed or was doing a good job of covering his nerves.

"Okay, just wondering."

"Why? Is something wrong?"

"I hope not." Not wanting to give Bernie the opportunity to probe further, she said, "I think I'll go out and see how it's going with Mac."

"Yes, ma'am. And I'll get at the colt's stall so it's done before McKenna's finished with him."

Though his initial reaction still bothered her, Cat told herself to forget it. Bernie had probably been afraid she'd thought he'd done something wrong.

Out back, Aidan and Mac were in the round pen. On foot, Mac moved in a smooth circle. It wasn't until she got to the fence and stepped up on the lower board that she had a clear view of owner and horse turning together as a team. Aidan stayed slightly behind Mac's shoulder, and when he turned in the opposite direction, so did Mac.

Only, Aidan wasn't using a lunge whip or even a lunge line.

He wasn't using hand signals.

He wasn't even using his voice.

The two together were a beautiful thing to watch. Trainer and horse formed a real team, Mac working hard as if to please Aidan. Mac was one of the most magnificent pieces of horseflesh she'd ever had the pleasure of seeing. And Aidan was the most attractive man whose flesh she would like to see.

Shaking away the lascivious thought, Cat reminded herself she'd been through this already. The issue was settled. Wasn't it? Aidan was simply her business partner. She told herself she didn't need him to be more than that.

But the magic she was watching felt incredibly seductive to a woman who lived and breathed to make beautiful foals that grew into magnificent horses, while Aidan lived and breathed to train them to be champions.

At that moment, Cat thought she might be just a tiny bit in love with Aidan.

The balletic duo ended too soon. She'd gotten out to the barn too late to see the entire exercise.

Aidan walked over to her, Mac following like his big dark shadow.

"How do you do that?" she asked, noting how Mac caught up to Aidan and swung his head into his trainer's arm for some personal attention.

Aidan gave him a pat. "What exactly?"

"No lunge line. No voice. It's as if Mac Finnian anticipated your every move."

"Exactly." Mac jostled his arm again, more insistently this time, and Aidan reached into his pocket and pulled out a candy. "We have a special connection. We read each other without words."

Cat grinned as Aidan unwrapped a striped peppermint. Aidan offered it to Mac, who at the moment made her think of the dogs when they wanted a treat. They would pester her to death until she acquiesced.

Suddenly realizing Aidan's implication, she said, "Wait. Are you saying you have a *psychic* connection? With a horse?"

"Do you think it impossible?"

"I think it's a little out there, Aidan, but I'm sure you've heard that before." Something truly special had gone on between the two, but "psychic" was a little over the top. She sighed. "Jack used to talk like that. He told me all kinds of tales to charm me. Maybe he took all the magic out of my life."

"I'm not trying to charm you, and I'm not your ex-husband."

He sounded ticked, Cat thought. And he was charming her whether or not he knew it. "Okay, fair enough." Let him have his fantasy. It didn't hurt anyone.

"Believe me when I tell you I just know what Mac wants, and he knows what I want from him. I'm a McKenna from a family of McKennas who have…well… certain abilities. My immediate family all have different abilities with horses and other animals."

The way Mac was shouldering Aidan, hanging his head over the trainer's, Cat could believe he and the colt had a link of some kind, even if there was nothing supernatural about it. "A lot of trainers claim a special connection to their horses. What makes your relationship with Mac any different?"

"I know what he's thinking."

Back to the psychic claim. She laughed. "Okay, I'll go along with it."

Aidan's expression closed a bit. "Well, you shall just have to see for yourself, will you not? C'mon, lad, let's get you moving for a bit. Don't want you to cool down now that you're ready to work."

Cat realized she'd been dismissed because she hadn't taken Aidan seriously. Surely he hadn't thought she really would believe the tale.

He began circling the round pen at a walk, Mac accompanying him, sticking to his side as if he were Aidan's companion. Like one of the dogs, she thought again, though neither Smokey nor Topaz would stay by her side for this long. Curiosity would get the better of them and they would run off to investigate any movement or smell. Watching horse and man so connected enthralled her.

Noting the saddle and accompanying tack stacked on a nearby equipment storage box, and reluctant to go back inside the barn, Cat asked, "Are you going to take Mac out on the training track?"

"Aye. It has been a few weeks since he was able

to really stretch his legs." Aidan moved to the gate. "He's ready to race."

As Cat saw for herself ten minutes later.

Once tacked up and on the track near the wheeled two-stall starting gate that took up a quarter of the track's width, Mac started to dance. Aidan mounted him and walked the colt to familiarize him with the foreign surface. And undoubtedly to make certain he was properly warmed up before running, Cat thought.

"The track is five furlongs," she told him. "Do you think he'd be all right if you took him around twice?" Ten furlongs was a mile and a quarter, the length of the Breeders' Cup Classic.

"Aye, but I'm not going to push him just yet," Aidan said. "I intend to breeze Mac and if he wants to go farther, then let him set his own pace. Let himself decide if he wants to go the distance."

Appreciating Aidan's care for the colt's potential stress in a new environment, Cat settled down to watch as he lined Mac up alongside the starting gate with the same effortless power as before.

What would it be like to be with a man who possessed that kind of power? How would he use that power on her?

With a silent signal from Aidan, Mac broke from his position and Cat caught her breath as the colt's musculature bunched and released. Mesmerized, she barely blinked as he rounded the track.

He passed the gate once. Dirt spewed around him and he picked up speed as he rounded the track the second time. The colt's pace was so fast she fancied he had the wind under his hooves. She swore he made the second lap seem easier than the first. He breezed by the starting gate as if ready to do another five furlongs.

Aidan let the colt slow to a trot, then turned him to come back to where Cat waited near the starting gate.

"Mac looks like a champion to me," she said, unable to contain her excitement.

"He was simply shedding his travel stress. Just think of what he can do without a heavy bloke like me in the saddle."

Cat didn't know exactly what Aidan weighed, but she guessed he was about fifty or sixty pounds heavier than the average jockey. Less weight on the colt's back would mean a big gain in speed. Assuming Mac made it to the Classic, he would carry only 126 pounds including the saddle.

She couldn't wait to see how fast Mac's first workout would be when he had a much lighter exercise rider on his back.

Her hopes that Mac had it in him to be a champion soared.

## *Chapter Seven*

Something about Dr. Helen Fox brought Pegeen to Aidan's mind. Taking care of Mac, he'd gotten a glimpse of the vet as she entered the barn with Cat. There was the fiery hair, of course, which made him wonder if she had more than that in common with his late lover. As he groomed Mac in the next aisle, he listened. The way the vet approached the mares as she checked them over convinced him of her capability, but something off—an odd vibe he got from her—made him want to know more about her. He was finishing with Mac when Dean Hill swept in. Aidan quietly followed, entering the aisle holding Hill's broodmares, simply to appease his curiosity.

Cat stood with Hill and the vet, and seeing her happy and smiling suddenly made him uncomfortable. Wanting her suddenly made guilt course through him.

"So what's the verdict on Fairy Tail?" Hill demanded.

"I checked on her, but it's too soon to tell," the vet replied. "Give it another day or two."

"You'd think a good vet would be able to tell more quickly."

The vet narrowed her gaze on him. "You'd think an owner would be pleased two of his mares conceived so quickly."

Her cheeky comment to the man who paid her to care for his mares raised Aidan's eyebrows. But Hill immediately backed down into apologetic mode.

"Of course I am pleased. I'm just excited to finally see foals sired by False Promise. Best damn horse I ever owned. His breaking down before he reached his true potential bollixed my racing plans, and I'm overly anxious to get back on the track with a future champion." He barked a laugh. "Think of me as a potential new father waiting to hand out the cigars."

Aidan understood Hill's anxiousness, but the reality of the matter was that he would have to be patient for three years before he could race a foal conceived this summer.

"The rewards will be worth the wait," the vet said.

Her smile looked forced. Did she not like Hill for some reason? Aidan wondered. Or was that vibe he'd sensed more telling about her openness?

"I need to get back to my place," Hill told Cat. "Let me know if anything changes."

"Of course. Diamond Dame may be ready for cover by tomorrow. If so, will you be here?"

"Depends. I might be involved in something. Just keep me informed."

Hill departed, nodding to Aidan as he passed him.

"Are you waiting for me?" the vet suddenly asked, as if she just spotted him leaning against a stall wall.

Aidan took the opportunity. "I thought we should meet. I may be in need of your services."

"Is something wrong with Mac?" The color drained from Cat's face.

"Nah, nah." Aidan stepped forward. "I simply thought since the good doctor was here, that it would be a grand time to introduce myself."

He held out his hand and the vet hesitated a moment before taking it. "Dr. Helen Fox."

At the first touch, Aidan started. He saw through the vet's smile, realized she was forcing it as she had for Hill. Any resemblance to Pegeen lay strictly in the hair. Pegeen had been open and vibrant. Dr. Helen Fox held herself tight, at least with people. But he sensed there was more… something unsettling…something elusive that he still couldn't pin down.

"So you're the Irishman with the really fast horse."

"That I am. Mac Finnian would be his name."

"I'll remember that. I wish you luck."

The vet said the words like she meant them, but did she? Why did Aidan get the feeling she was simply saying what he expected to hear? Though his true ability was with horses, he could often read people, too.

"What time do you want to leave for the track?" he asked Cat.

"Not until 3:30. We have plenty of time. Helen and I need to take a look at the new mare Martin Bradley brought in yesterday. How about getting something to eat in about a half hour and then taking a trail ride?"

Hesitant at spending so much time alone with her—he hadn't forgotten what had almost happened between them the night before—he said, "We could do it another day when you've had more rest."

Color flooded her face, but she didn't back down. "Being on horseback is the ideal way to familiarize yourself with the property and surroundings."

"Good point. If you are certain—"

"Positive. We're almost through here."

"Take her up on the offer," the vet said. "This

is the most beautiful time of the year to explore on horseback."

"Well, then, on horseback it is."

An hour later, they set off together on two of Cat's geldings—her on a chestnut, him on a bay—Cat's dogs accompanying them.

Already a little homesick, Aidan couldn't help but admire the natural beauty of the land, the pristine condition of the pastures, as they rode along the far fence. "'Tis a beautiful place you have here."

"Thanks, but you have to give my parents the credit. They turned the old Clarke family farm into the breeding facility that Clarke Acres is today. I didn't have a thing to do with it. All that work went into the place before I was even a sparkle in Mom's eye. When Dad retired, they simply handed over the reins to me."

"But you maintain their work in a grand manner. They must be very proud of you."

"I like to think so. I love this place and never want to be anywhere else. I know how Dad feels, how much he misses doing the work. I see it in his face every time my parents visit."

Aidan wished his parents were equally interested in what he and his brothers did. They'd started in the racing game despite their father's very vocal disapproval. The McKennas had always owned land and horses, but for pleasure riding only. Their parents would have had their three sons all be professional men—meaning working in offices that would have choked their spirits. For their own good, of course. Aidan knew his parents loved all three of their sons even if they didn't understand them.

He and Cashel and Tiernan had spent their boyhoods plotting and planning. Even then they'd known they'd wanted to be horsemen.

Suddenly Cat stopped her horse and dismounted.

"Is something wrong?"

"Just turning off the electric fence so the dogs can come off the property. I'm going to take you on the forest preserve trails—they start only a few minutes' ride from here."

"Lovely," he said, meaning her as well as the anticipation of an unexpected adventure.

The way she looked…the way she moved…the way she kissed with such passion…

Guilt licked at him. How could he be so attracted to another lass when he hadn't forgotten Pegeen? Not that he wanted to forget her. Or replace her.

Still, no harm in looking. Or admiring. As long as that was all it was…

"Okay," Cat said, "we're good to go."

The dogs, undoubtedly ecstatic to be off the

more familiar property into new territory, led the way.

"I haven't been out here for more than a month," Cat said. "The spring rains have done their job. Everything is so lush now."

They followed a line of trees marking the end of Clarke Acres property at an easy lope, going from open pastureland to forest within a few minutes. The dogs zigzagged back and forth, alternately exploring and checking on the humans. Eventually, the riding path split. Cat took the one where the land sloped and twisted and turned. They slowed the horses to a walk and traversed the narrow path above a ravine and the creek beyond.

Aidan noted they hadn't seen another soul.

A short while later, Cat took him off the trail into a thickly forested area, where the horses carefully picked their way between trees until they came into a little clearing with a fire pit and downed trees as seating. They were directly above the creek. The dogs shot ahead to explore again.

"'Tis like being in a paradise of our own."

"Today." She dismounted, let her horse get some water. "You wouldn't want to be out here on a weekend. Anyone who owns a horse would probably be on the trail."

But they weren't on the trail anymore. Following her lead, Aidan dismounted as well, one thing on his mind.

Her. Naked.

What did he have to do to stop himself from thinking like that?

"I'll take paradise when I can get it, then," he said, rubbing his mount's ears and giving him silent instructions to stay put.

Cat was watching him closely. Her gaze burned into him, and his flesh responded instantly. Unable to help himself, he dropped the reins and stepped toward her.

"What are you doing?" she asked, the words coming out in a gasp.

Her eyes were wide, her lips parted in invitation.

As hard as he tried, he couldn't stop himself. This time he kissed her.

She dropped her horse's reins and wound her arms around his neck to pull him closer.

Cupping both breasts, he backed her against a fallen tree that hit her at hip level. He circled her nipples until they hardened to small peaks. She moaned but didn't object. Instead, she began exploring him.

This was a bad idea.

He knew it was a bad idea and had vowed not to let it happen.

At the moment, he simply didn't care.

Within seconds they were undoing each other's belt buckles, snaps and zippers. He slipped his hand into her pants, into her. She felt so hot and swollen and wet.

Her hands on his hard flesh…he didn't know how long he could stand it.

He broke the kiss, whispered in her ear. "Are we really doing this?"

"It's just sex."

The right response. *Just sex.*

No emotional involvement.

No betrayal of a memory.

No taunting a curse.

The curse was well and done anyway, Aidan reminded himself, had been fulfilled with Pegeen's death.

Just sex, he thought, as they pulled down each other's jeans in unison. Trying to take her like this was awkward. They'd have to take off their boots and the clothing puddling around their knees. Unless…

He turned her so she faced the log. She draped herself over it and he draped himself over her.

She was so wet, he slid into her easily from behind, so swollen she held on to him like a tight fist. Knowing he wouldn't have long, he trailed his lips up her arm and lightly bit the soft flesh of her shoulder while forcing a hand in front of her to touch and tease and torment her until she was breathing heavy.

Panting.

Murmuring, “Now…now…now!”

Her plea inflamed him. He plunged deeper and faster and within a few strokes, her strangled sounds forced him over the edge.

She cried in pleasure, then whispered something that sounded like “I needed that.”

That made two of them, he thought, now using his hands on the tree to steady himself. His legs felt like rubber.

He’d dreamed this after they’d met. His gut tightened and he took a deep breath to control the panic hiding a nick away.

Just sex.

Very clear-cut. No emotional entanglement.

Still, as he backed off, he couldn’t take his eyes off Cat. Her face was flushed and still marked with seduction. His physical response surprised him, considering he’d just finished, but she had already dressed. What could have been an awkward moment wasn’t. She didn’t avoid his eyes. She met them. Held them. A knowing smile played around her lips.

Knowing or promising?

The dogs barking from somewhere nearby broke the tension. Aidan realized they’d been barking earlier, but they’d been so physically involved that the source of the noise hadn’t registered.

“I think we should get going,” Cat said, brushing by him in a way that made him want to convince her they needn't rush.

But before he could do anything about it, she mounted her horse. He took her cue and followed. She moved her horse uphill, back to the trail, and whistled for the dogs, but they continued to kick up a fuss.

Now Cat looked concerned as she focused on a spot ahead and halfway down the ravine. "What are they doing, going way down there?" She gave them another sharp whistle but they didn't stop. "Smokey! Topaz! Come back, now!"

The dogs ignored her. They didn't slow until they reached the bottom of the ravine. The barking took a more frantic tone.

If he wasn't mistaken, it sounded as if they were calling Cat, Aidan thought, concentrating and tuning out everything but their high-pitched voices. Though he mostly had experience communicating with horses, it wasn't all that hard to read the dogs. They were telling her to come look at what they'd found, and it wasn't anything good.

"Probably a dead animal," Cat said, then whistled for the dogs again.

For a moment, Aidan thought they would come, but they stood their ground. Topaz started whining. Smokey started digging.

"All right, I'm going have to go see what big

discovery they made." She groaned. "I'm sure it'll be something disgusting."

Cat edged her mount off the path and zigzagged down the ravine. Feeling oddly tense, Aidan followed. Something about the tone of the dogs' voices got to him deep in his core. Remembering the night's dream that had kept him awake until dawn, he knew this wasn't good.

Both dogs were digging now, making whining noises that made it sound as if they were crying. This wasn't a fun find for them. The dogs were freaked out and, his gut clenching, Aidan was certain he knew why.

When they got to the bottom of the ravine, Aidan felt as if he was experiencing this for the second time.

As if last night's rain had bloated the creek to overflow its banks and wash away the earth to expose it, a man's booted foot stuck out of the ground.

Then Cat yelped and jumped off her horse and ran to the dogs, who were digging furiously. Aidan dismounted and joined her, put an arm around her back to support her as they got a better look at what Smokey and Topaz uncovered—a bloated face, skin tinged a green-blue and blistered, tongue protruding, fluid oozing from the mouth and nostrils, maggots eating their way through the side of the dead man's head where it had been opened by some heavy object.

Cat let out a horrific cry and clung to him. His instinct to protect her made Aidan hold her close as he said a silent prayer for the dead man at their feet.

"I knew it," she said, her tone ripe with horror. Her fingers dug into the flesh of his arms, as if she needed to anchor herself to him. "I knew something was wrong, but no one believed me."

"I don't understand. You recognize the man?"

"This is my missing barn manager." She choked out the words. "George Odell."

## *Chapter Eight*

"He would have been in a state of deterioration that would have made him unrecognizable if whoever killed him hadn't buried him," Detective Wade Pierce said when they convened in Cat's kitchen two hours later. "Three weeks exposed to the air and—"

"Please. What we saw was horrific enough," Aidan said.

Guilt crept up Cat's spine. Not the guilt of having sex with a man she hardly knew, but having it within a hundred yards of a dead man she'd known all her life. She made fists in her lap as she thought about what they'd been doing when the dogs had made the initial discovery. Not exactly a way she would have chosen to honor George. Her eyes stung with unshed tears. She couldn't have known, of course, but that didn't make her feel any better.

All these weeks…she should have suspected her barn manager was dead…should have investigated herself…should have found his remains before anything happened between her and Aidan. Seeing him that way right after having exciting, heart-pounding sex…

Cat swallowed hard.

She'd thought having sex with another man would obliterate any memories of Jack from her mind. And now she didn't know if she could ever have sex again.

"Who could have done this?" she whispered.

Pierce said, "Hopefully my men will get a lead from something in his trailer."

Sitting across the table from him, Cat made eye contact with the trim and fit if seasoned detective, who looked to be in his early fifties by the creases in his face.

"I knew something was wrong when George disappeared. I made a complaint to your department," she reminded Pierce in a forced-steady voice, "but no one would believe me."

"I remember. I also remember asking if you knew who had something against him and you didn't have any reason to believe there was foul play. Any new thoughts there?"

George's body had already been taken to the morgue, though the evidence technicians were still investigating the burial site. She and Aidan had already told the detective in detail how they'd found the body. Just not what they'd been doing while the dogs had been investigating.

She shook her head. "In the past three weeks, I've gone over and over what could have happened to make him simply vanish. I got nothing. George was a sweetheart and a hard worker and he kept to himself mostly."

"What about when he had to deal with other people? He was your barn manager, after all. What about his relationship with your other workers?"

Cat didn't want to believe one of her farm employees was capable of murder. She met Aidan's gaze. He gave her an encouraging nod and placed a reassuring hand over hers.

Biting back the tears she wanted to shed, Cat said, "He got along with them fine. Mostly."

"What do you mean by 'mostly'?"

"Like you said, he was my barn manager. Sometimes he had to ride a little hard on someone to make sure the work got done."

"Ride on who?" Pierce asked. "The kids?"

"Vincent and Laura? Yeah, sure, once in a while, but they want to be here. In addition to their wages, they get to take out the horses on the trails when their work is done, so they went out of their way to please George."

"What about your men, Ayala and Hansen?"

"Raul's a good worker. Bernie, too, but he's

young. He didn't like being bossed around, that's all."

"Any real altercations?"

"Physical? No, of course not. Just a few arguments about how Bernie did things. George thought Bernie cut too many corners." Unable to sit any longer, Cat got to her feet and moved to the sink where she turned her back on the men and quickly swiped the moisture from her eyes. "I would swear George didn't have an enemy in the world."

"Obviously he had one," Aidan said.

Cat's stomach clutched as she remembered the shocking way they'd discovered the body, the sickening sight of the bashed-in head. If Aidan hadn't been there for support, both moral and physical, she didn't know how she would have gotten through this.

Scribbling something in his notebook, Pierce then turned his gaze on the Irishman. "What about you, Mr. McKenna? Any thoughts?"

Aidan shrugged. "I didn't even know the man. I only arrived here in Illinois yesterday."

"To what purpose?"

"To race my colt, Mac Finnian. He's in the stable now." Aidan checked his watch. "As a matter of fact, we're due at the track to get everything set up for his move there in a little more than an hour. Should one of us call and reschedule for tomorrow?"

"I don't see that'll be necessary." Detective Pierce thought for a moment, then mused, "Odd that you found the victim at all, considering where he was buried."

"Cat was simply showing me the lay of the land. 'Twas the dogs who found him, as we told you," Aidan said. "They wouldn't come to her command, so she went to fetch them or we wouldn't have found the body and the man's whereabouts would still be a mystery."

Pierce nodded and put away his notebook.

"The question is," Aidan went on, "where was the man killed? Surely not in the ravine. A convenient place to bury him, but what would he have been doing out there in the first place?"

"Well, that would be the question, wouldn't it?"

"That didn't even occur to me." Cat didn't want to consider George might have been killed somewhere on the farm. "He could have been killed anywhere. Even in town."

"Quite right." Pierce got up to leave. "That'll be all for now."

Staring out the kitchen window, Cat saw Laura and Vincent outside the barn, police officers rushing around them. Laura was crying and Vincent was trying to console her. He wrapped his arms around the girl as she sobbed into his chest. His expression told Cat he was ready to break down himself. She felt sorry for the kids—they were so young, they couldn't hide their grief at losing someone to whom they'd been so close.

"Anything we can do for you, Detective," Aidan was saying.

"I want to see what we come up with—if anything. Then talk to your workers—"

"Not the kids," Cat said. Laura was upset enough.

"Everyone. The kids might have noticed something important. That includes the owners who have their stock stabled here, by the way. Dean Hill is one of them, right?"

Cat nodded. "He's here for the long haul. His horses will be here until after they foal, at least. Martin Bradley has several mares here, but that's only until they conceive." And if Jack really went through with his plan to give his fiancée the broodmares he'd taken from her, Martin would undoubtedly want to bring in even more. "Hershel Miller and Audrey Rockwell have a couple of mares here to be bred, as well."

Several new broodmares were scheduled to come to be covered in the following week. At least she hoped their owners wouldn't change their minds—one never knew what damage gossip would do.

Speaking of damage…Cat couldn't believe it

when the red truck pulled up outside. Oh, great. Jack. Just what she needed. Her ex-husband certainly knew how to make an entrance at the worst times. Had he already heard about George and was here to put in his two cents? She closed her eyes and collected herself—she wouldn't let Jack make her break down in tears. She wouldn't.

"You never know what they might have noticed that you didn't," Pierce said. "Plus I'm going to do some asking around town."

Thinking he should have done that three weeks ago when she first reported George missing, Cat clenched her jaw. She didn't have to like it, but she could see his side of the matter.

"We'll talk again," Pierce promised. "Soon."

Cat escorted the detective out of the house, satisfied that she'd gotten her emotions under control. Aidan followed close behind her. She wished he would take a step back. If Pierce noticed how protective he was being, she didn't want to have to explain herself. Not that what she did, or with whom, was any of his business.

Nor was it Jack's.

Her ex-husband stomped into the middle of things. "What's going on here?"

Cat kept her focus on Pierce, who stopped at his vehicle. "So you'll keep me informed, right?"

"As much as I can." He opened the car door.

"Gonna drive over to the trailer. Got a corn that's practically killing me." Pierce jiggled his right foot.

"Hey, I asked a question." Jack appeared to be fuming at being ignored. "Detective Pierce?"

Pierce looked from Jack to Cat, who couldn't hide her displeasure.

"How well did you know George Odell?" he asked her ex-husband.

"Well, enough, I guess. I did live here for more than a year. You still didn't answer my question."

Pierce continued his interrogation. "How well did you get along with Odell?"

"I don't form relationships with the hired help."

"Because they don't have money or influence," Cat added.

Before Jack could jump on her, Pierce asked, "Does that mean you didn't get along?"

"Why do I get the feeling you're not telling me something I should know?" Jack demanded.

"George Odell is dead."

Jack shrugged. "Too bad, but he was old, lived a good life."

Shocked at his attitude, Cat stared, open-mouthed.

Then Aidan said, "He was murdered."

Cat glanced at him. His gaze was glued to her ex-husband.

Jack didn't react for a moment, then exploded.

"Wait a minute—you don't think I had anything to do with it?" He turned a furious expression on Cat. "What have you been telling these men? Are you trying to get even with me because I left you for another woman?"

"Your name never even came up, Jack," Cat assured him. But maybe it should have. "George disappeared before I was called back from Ireland to meet you in divorce court."

"So what?"

"So you took as much as you could from me. How do I know you weren't snooping around the farm, seeing what you could put your hands on? Maybe George caught you and you—"

"Bitch!" Jack yelled, stepping toward Cat threateningly.

Aidan got between them. "That'll be enough now. Cat doesn't need you giving her more trouble."

"Who the hell do you think you are?"

"A friend of the lass. I would not threaten her if I were you."

"All right, all right, let's just calm down here," Pierce said, then turned to Jack. "What about it? Were you here at Clarke Acres while your ex-wife was in Ireland?"

"She was still my wife then."

"Not so as anyone would know it," Cat said.

"Were you here?" Pierce repeated.

"Yeah, once. I had a right to be here, since we were still married. I didn't want her trying to put one over on me in court, so I was checking things out for myself. I figured if she was out of the country on a buying trip, she had more assets than I realized. But I didn't kill George. Never even saw him."

Only once? Knowing how easily lies tripped off his lips, Cat would be surprised if that was the truth.

"Who did you see?" Pierce asked.

"Bernie. He can vouch for me. I was only here for half an hour."

Having expected him to say *Martin Bradley,* Cat started.

"I'll check with him about it," the detective said, getting into his vehicle. "In the meantime, take McKenna's advice and back off."

He headed the car for the other side of the barn where the trailers were located.

"I would suggest you leave now," Aidan told Jack.

"This isn't your property!"

Aidan turned to Cat. "Do you want him here?"

"No. Leave, Jack. Now."

Aidan got right up in Jack's face. "You heard the lass."

Cat watched breathlessly to see what her ex-husband would do. The men engaged in a staring match that seemed to go on forever. To her satisfaction, Jack looked away first.

"Our business isn't settled," he warned her, as he made for his shiny new red truck.

Cat didn't bother answering him lest he warm up to the argument and torture her further.

"Thank you," she murmured, as the truck's wheels spun gravel. Earlier she'd been comparing him to Jack because of the money issue, but at the moment it seemed they were nothing alike. Aidan had taken a stand to protect her. "I don't think I could have gone another round with him today."

"At your service," Aidan said. "Anytime."

Cat swallowed hard. Only here two days, and Aidan had become a complication that she wasn't sure she wanted.

How the hell had they found George Odell's body? They'd taken it out deep into the woods, had buried it in a steep ravine way off the trail near the creek.

Damn dogs.

At least they hadn't found the suitcase.

He'd been careful to pack just enough clothes to make everyone believe George had gone somewhere on a whim and would be back shortly. No one would have ever guessed he was dead and buried.

Good thing they hadn't buried the suitcase with him.

Good thing he'd thought to wipe it down, get rid of his fingerprints.

Good thing he'd had the sense to fling it into the creek.

Undoubtedly the suitcase had been washed away and was miles from here by now, maybe had landed in one of the little lakes that dotted this part of the state. The police would never find it.

But they'd be looking.

He felt his nerves fray. They'd be looking not only for the suitcase, but for any kind of clue to George's murder.

His stomach churned and bile filled his esophagus. He pulled some antacids from his pocket and chewed them.

How had this happened? He hadn't meant for anyone to die.

Swallowing hard, he told himself again that he wasn't really a murderer. He hadn't planned it. He'd simply done what he had to do to protect himself, was all. Not that the police would understand.

They'd be talking to people, too.

Only one other person knew *how* George had died. Only two people other than he would know *why* the barn manager had died.

Now he had them to worry about. Would they keep their mouths shut? What if they shared what they knew with someone else?

Another shot of bile made it into his mouth. He took out more antacid. As long as no one had been asking questions, he'd figured he'd be safe.

They'd now be asking questions of everyone who knew George.

Could he trust his two partners in crime to keep their mouths shut?

If they didn't, they'd be implicated, too, he thought. They could be arrested and serve time, so why wouldn't they keep silent?

*What if one of them wanted to make a deal in lieu of a sentence?* a little voice asked.

He was the one with blood on his hands.

He shoved his hands in his pockets to hide them, told himself to stop obsessing before he went out of his mind.

He would do whatever it took to protect himself.

Protecting himself—and the money—that was all that mattered.

## *Chapter Nine*

Their appointment at McHenry Racecourse to tour the facility and to get their stall assignment for Mac was coming up fast, so after the other men left, Aidan had just enough time to shower. He threw on fresh clothes and pulled his fingers through his hair, then went upstairs.

Cat was waiting for him in the kitchen. She'd been so stoic with Pierce and her ex-husband, but he now caught her in a weak moment. Her reddened eyes and nose were proof that she'd been crying. He wanted in the worst way to take her in his arms, reassure her that everything would be all right.

Not that it would.

Dead was dead, as he well knew. He still carried sorrow after the better part of a year. The grief had faded, true, and he didn't think of Pegeen as often as he had in those first crippling months, but considering the way she'd died, he wouldn't ever be able to forget.

And from the way Cat drew herself up and put her expression in neutral, he didn't think she was going to share her grief with him.

"I can go to the track alone," he said. "'Tis been a terrible day and you could use some rest."

"I want to go."

"No need, Cat. Simply give me directions and allow me to drive your vehicle."

"Going to the track will give me something… something else to think about."

"You're certain?"

She stood tall, her chin lifted. "I need this, Aidan."

Even as he noted her lower lip quiver, he said, "Aye. Let us go, then." Perhaps she was correct and did need to get away from the farm, if only for a bit.

They set off for the track with Cat driving her SUV. Aidan's good mood after Mac's first workout had been ruined by their find in the woods. Now he was worrying about the lass because she drove in silence. It wasn't simply the shock of finding the man dead that had gotten to her, he knew. There was more to it.

"Do you want to talk about it?" he asked.

"Not right now."

Her voice sounded a bit choked as if she was preventing herself from crying again.

Aidan couldn't help himself. "I don't mean the

way we found the man, but about how you felt for him."

Cat's hands tightened on the steering wheel so that her knuckles went white.

He was trying to think of a safer topic, when she said, "George was like part of my family. Like an uncle, I think I told you. I don't ever remember him not being there. He taught me to tack my pony when I was little and my parents were too busy. I used to follow him around the barn when I was a kid, asking him a million qu-questions." Her voice broke and she went silent for a moment before continuing. "He never got annoyed with me, always treated me like I was an adult. He even warned me about Jack."

"He didn't like your ex-husband, then?"

"George saw Jack for what he was—an opportunist and a clever liar."

"He lied to you?"

"To get me to do what he wanted when he wanted—yes. Apparently more than I ever knew. I hated that I let him manipulate me like that. George never let on except in private, though. I didn't want to believe it, of course. I thought we were in love, and I needed someone to support me. I don't think Jack ever realized how George felt about him."

"Or maybe he did," Aidan mused. Could he

have blamed the barn manager for opening Cat's eyes to him?

"Jack is a lot of things, but he's not a murderer. At least I hope not. If so, then George's death *was* my fault. Bad enough that he turned out to be such a bastard."

Aidan hoped she was correct about her ex-husband, because if she wasn't, she could be in danger, as well. Suddenly realizing that he felt something for Cat, more than he'd previously wanted to face, Aidan sat stunned. That Cat was hurting made him want to make it all better. Not that he could. A man was dead. Murdered. Nothing was going to make her feel better about that.

Nothing was going to make him feel better that he couldn't help her.

How had that happened? He'd never denied Cat was attractive, but her sudden testiness at that first meeting had put him off. There were the dreams, of course, but there was also Pegeen's ghost sitting on his shoulder, reminding him of what he'd lost and why.

The unexpected hot kiss the night before had done it, had turned him around. Though he'd been the one to break it off, Aidan hadn't been able to forget it.

Despite the dream that had warned him, having sex in the woods had still been unexpected and exciting, and now, sitting beside her in her SUV, he had to play mind games with himself so he didn't obsess over it.

While Cat was understandably upset about her barn manager's death, she didn't seem to have any residual tension about what had happened between them.

Not like he did.

Thinking they could both use a break from the horror of finding the dead man, he asked, "Are you familiar with the backstretch at McHenry?"

"I've never raced a colt or filly of my own, but I've been back there with a couple of clients, usually when they were thinking of retiring a mare to breed her."

"But 'tis decent?"

"Well…the shedrows are well taken care of," she said, a hesitant note in her voice. "The living quarters are the usual dormitories now, but management has plans for new construction, including apartments with kitchenettes."

"So the backstretch workers can bring their families to live with them. As it should be."

He was glad to hear it. Tracks normally had only single rooms shared by two or more workers with public toilets on each floor. Like living in a school dormitory, only the workers had to supply their own bedding, which often was nothing more than a cot or a sleeping bag. Most workers were transient, going from track to track with the trainers, but still, that was no reason not to give them a decent place to live.

Aidan knew McHenry had upgraded its racing schedule in the past few years, as well, adding several graded races, the first of which was the stakes race coming up in less than two weeks now. He was counting on Mac to win and take the first step in his and Cashel's plan for the colt. And Cat's, he amended. He couldn't forget the woman who'd made this possible.

Glancing her way, flashing on the heat they'd shared, he thought Cat Clarke would be impossible to forget under any circumstance.

"The only thing I'm worried about is getting the right jockey," Aidan said.

"Time's a little tight, but we can fly someone in if we have to."

"I would rather meet the man in person before making a decision."

Aidan trusted his gut instinct—and that of whatever horse he was training—more than simple statistics. He liked to put jockey and horse together and to get a read off the match before hiring anyone. His method had served him well. More than once in his career, he'd sensed an uneasiness in the colt or filly when introducing them to a potential jockey and had gone on to interview another candidate. The result—success.

They reached the racecourse situated right off

the interstate. Cat drove past the grandstand to the back side of the track where the horses were stabled, trained and maintained. A guardhouse monitored the fenced backstretch. They had to show identification to get in. The area housed a practice track and dozens of buildings—Aidan noted shedrows, dormitories, blacksmith, cafeteria, a coin-operated Laundromat, and even a medical clinic to treat illnesses as well as the injuries that were common to those working with horses. Aidan would have to familiarize himself with a whole host of support staff, since backstretch workers included exercise riders, grooms, farriers and muckers, among others.

They parked outside the office and headed straight in. The manager made sure their paperwork was in order. When Cat pulled out her cell phone to make a call, her hand shook a little. Aidan worried about her as she took care of his trainer's license. Somehow, she kept herself pulled together.

Then they were introduced to a young exercise rider who wanted to work with him. Short and slender but muscular, Nadim could be a jockey. Perhaps that was his goal, Aidan thought. Many jockeys started in the business as exercise riders. Nadim was probably only eighteen or nineteen.

"I'll give you the whole tour," the lad said. "Take you around the grounds and introduce you to some of the people. You already have your stall assignment, so we'll start there."

They headed from the office straight for it, Nadim keeping up the chatter as they walked.

"We have fifteen barns, more than a thousand horses stabled here. Workouts on the main track are the standard 6:00 a.m. until 10:00 a.m. After that, you have to move onto the practice track."

"What about guests or bringing my own workers in?" Cat asked.

Aidan realized she really didn't know about the workings of the backstretch.

"Workers have to be licensed first," Nadim said. "No guests unless they're cleared and you get a badge ahead of time."

And on he went.

Sneaking looks at Cat, he noted she alternated between strong and emotional, though she did her best to hide the latter. They soon arrived at the shedrow that would house Mac.

Aidan was pleased to see that it was closest to the grandstand, an area away from the hustle and bustle of the track's backside and therefore as quiet as it was possible to get. Two rows of two dozen stalls faced each other, a twelve-foot-wide covered walkway in between. Though a worker watered a basket of flowers hanging from a hook at the end of the building, oddly, the stalls on one side were empty of horses. Inside the stall assigned to them, another worker was taking apart a ceiling light.

"The stall will be available tomorrow," Nadim said. "We're just doing some maintenance checks. There was a problem with the electrical in this shedrow. We want to check all the fixtures and circuits before reopening the stalls to horses."

"Good," Cat said, her voice a bit flat. "I'm glad someone is on top of that."

The biggest fear in any barn being fire, Aidan knew.

Cat seemed distracted, as if she couldn't quite concentrate. Despite the trauma of finding her late barn manager, she was holding up better than Aidan had expected. He wanted to get this over as quickly as possible and get her home where she could grieve in private.

"I assume this is satisfactory, Mr. McKenna?"

Aidan started. "Aye, it'll do quite nicely. Now as to hiring you as an exercise rider…well, that would be up to Mac."

"You let the colt decide?"

"As to who gets up on his back? Aye. His call. I shall let you know after he has a chance to meet you tomorrow."

"Uh, okay." Nadim was trying not to look confounded. "How, um, do you know if he likes someone or not?"

"Because I can read his mind, of course."

A cell phone rang and Nadim excused himself, stepping away from the structure. "I'll be just a moment."

Aidan realized Cat was searching through her shoulder bag, her expression one of frustration.

"Only a while longer," he assured her. "Then we can be out of here."

"Not until I find my own cell phone." Her eyes pooled once more, as if she were ready to weep over the possible loss. "I checked for messages while you were taking care of your license. It's not in my purse."

"Maybe 'tis in the office, where you were using it."

Blinking and taking a deep breath, she said, "I'm going to have to go back and check."

"I shall accompany you."

"No, really. I need a little time alone anyway."

Apparently she did. Aidan was certain if he tried to put his arms around her right now, she would pull away from him. "All right. Where shall we meet?"

"Do whatever you need to do. I'll find you. If I have my cell, I can just call."

Nadim rejoined them. "The cafeteria?" he suggested, deferring to Aidan.

"Grand."

Cat said, "I'll meet you there, then." Avoiding his eyes, she rushed away.

Aidan couldn't take his gaze off her. She suddenly looked ready to crumble and he thought about going after her. Perhaps her being alone wasn't such a good idea, after all. She needed someone to lean on, and he couldn't think of anything he wanted more at the moment than to be her support.

And then Nadim brought him back to the reason he was there. "The cafeteria is in the middle of the backstretch."

Cat had already disappeared, so he decided to give her some time alone as she'd asked. He followed Nadim, only half-hearing the exercise rider giving him information on where to find what. He couldn't channel his worry for Cat.

Not until a weird sensation crept through him. He looked around to see a slightly built young man wearing sunglasses and a billed cap staring after him. Another exercise rider? There was something familiar about the lad, Aidan thought. As if he should know him. But he didn't know anyone here in America. Could this be someone he'd met at a track in Ireland or in England? Were other foreign horses stabled here?

"Are you acquainted with that man?" he asked Nadim, indicating the exercise rider should look back.

Nadim glanced over his shoulder. "Who?"

Aidan looked again.

The man was gone.

RELIEVED THAT SHE'D found her cell phone—apparently it had slipped from her purse onto the floor—Cat headed out of the office.

Her thoughts were scattered, fond memories of George interspersed with the image of him dead replaying in her mind over and over.

She'd told herself she would be okay coming out here, that she needed a distraction anyway. But all she wanted to do was head for home and have the privacy to shed more tears. Hopefully, that would be soon. She was tired of fighting her emotions. She didn't know how much longer she could keep her poker face. If, indeed, she'd even been presenting one.

She made for the cafeteria, but halfway there, she slowed when she caught sight of her ex-husband outside the laundry. She didn't need a second go-round with him in one afternoon. He was talking to Martin Bradley, his future father-in-law. Expressions serious, the men were deep in conversation. Like conspirators. Then Raul's young brother Placido, an up-and-coming jockey, left the laundry and joined them.

What was going on? Cat wondered as the three men walked off together.

After Jack had married her, he'd given up the

few horses he'd been training to "help" her run Clarke Acres.

Was he back in the game?

Was that why he'd gotten with Simone? So that her father would hire Jack to train some of his racehorses?

Or was something else at stake?

Thankful her ex-husband hadn't seen her, Cat backed off when they disappeared between buildings. She headed for the cafeteria, where she immediately spotted Aidan at a table with Nadim.

"Did you find your cell phone, then?" Aidan asked.

"I did, thankfully."

She slid into a chair next to him. Nadim was having coffee, Aidan a bottle of water.

"Can I get you something?" he asked.

"No, nothing for me, thanks. So?" She glanced from him to the exercise rider.

"I am more than happy to ride the colt in the morning workouts," Nadim said, "assuming he likes me." He turned to Aidan. "Assuming you hire me, I can find a groom and anyone else you need."

"Good," Cat said. "Then all we have to do is find the jockey."

Hopefully Aidan could do that himself when he moved Mac here, Cat thought. Her mind was drifting off. She longed to be out of here, back at her place, where she could mourn George in peace.

"You need a jockey, you don't have to look no further."

The voice coming from behind Cat made her start. "Placido." She looked around to see if Jack was there, too, but her ex-husband was nowhere in sight.

"Raul told me about Mac Finnian. Said maybe you'd give me the ride."

"Raul shouldn't have promised any such thing." Thinking again about seeing him with Jack and Martin, Cat looked to Aidan. "This is Placido Ayala, Raul's brother."

"Why should we consider you?" Aidan asked.

"Placido is an excellent candidate," Nadim said. "Last year, he was top jockey here, made the most money at this track."

"In the graded races?" Aidan asked.

"Some," Placido said. "I worked hard all winter, and I deserve a shot like this."

He was staring at *her,* as if she owed him something, Cat realized. "We haven't talked jockeys yet, Placido. We'll let you know."

"You'll hire me if you want to win the upcoming stakes race," Placido said before strolling off.

To her ears that sounded like a threat, rather than a promise.

Of course that was ridiculous. She hardly knew

Placido. He didn't come to the farm to see Raul very often, and she didn't hang out at the track. He had no reason to have something against her. It was just some macho posturing, she was sure.

"So I should meet you at the shedrow tomorrow at noon?" Nadim asked Aidan.

"That's the soonest we can get Mac in?"

"You can probably settle him in earlier. Call management and make certain the maintenance is finished."

Standing, Aidan offered the exercise rider his hand, and they shook on it. Cat was relieved that he was ready to go. This had been a difficult day and she wondered what more might be waiting for her when she got home.

As they walked to the car, Aidan asked, "What do you think about Placido as a jockey?"

"His record is good. Other than that, I don't know."

What she couldn't get out of mind was seeing him with Martin and Jack and then him approaching her, almost like Jack had put him up to it.

What could her ex-husband be up to now?

## *Chapter Ten*

The drive back to the farm was filled with silence. Cat appreciated Aidan letting her have time to chill out, but the first thing she looked for through the deepening gloom when she was back on her own property was police vehicles. Thankfully, they seemed to have all left.

She drove straight to the barn, and as she and Aidan got out of the SUV, Bernie came out to meet them.

"Police are gone," he said.

"Did they talk to everyone?" Cat asked. "The kids, too?"

"Yeah. And before he left, that detective guy said he was gonna talk to Mr. Hill and Mr. Bradley and the other owners. Said he'd be back."

"When?" Aidan sounded a bit apprehensive. "Tomorrow? Did they want us to be present?"

"Didn't say."

Cat knew Aidan was anxious about getting Mac settled at the track so he could start training him there, get him used to the new surroundings. "I assume they'll call if they want to interview us further," she said, "but I can't imagine why Pierce would need to question you again, Aidan, considering you didn't even know George and he disappeared weeks before you arrived."

"The detective seems to be a careful man," Aidan said.

"I hope so."

"Interviewing everyone, even the youngsters, searching the barn manager's trailer—"

"Pierce didn't really know George, either," she said. "What if he missed something important in the trailer?" Something she might spot as being out of place. "Maybe I should take a look myself."

She wanted in the worst way to simply put everything out of her mind for the moment and get a good night's sleep. Only she couldn't. Now that the idea had occurred to her, she wouldn't rest until she gave the trailer a thorough going-over.

"Um, do you need me for anything, Miss Clarke?" Bernie was shifting uncomfortably.

"Oh, no, Bernie. You can go back to whatever you were doing." She looked to Aidan. "I'll see you later."

Exhausted, she decided to drive to the trailer, though it wasn't all that far. Opening the vehicle door, she realized Aidan was getting in on the other side.

"Perhaps you can use a second pair of eyes on the place."

"Sure. That's a good idea. Thank you for offering."

Not that she would have asked Aidan to help her, but Cat was glad that he'd suggested doing so. He didn't have to do this, to get himself further involved in a murder, but she sensed that he had a code of honor that made him carry through. Or maybe he was simply being protective, considering the circumstances under which they'd discovered George's body. Either way, the comparison with Jack lost ground.

Cat imagined entering her barn manager's trailer would be one of the most difficult things she'd ever have to do. And a few minutes later, when they stood in front of the double-wide set off by itself in a copse of trees, she found she was correct. Reluctant to open the door, she was relieved when Aidan did it for her.

"I'll be going in first to make sure there are no more unpleasant surprises," he said.

A grateful Cat simply nodded.

Aidan was inside for less than a minute before he stepped back to the door and indicated she should come in.

The quarters that had always seemed so spacious for a trailer suddenly felt too cramped. Or perhaps Aidan was the problem. Cat was too aware of how close they were as they stood in the middle of the living area and looked around at the disarray. No doubt her discomfort came from the circumstances. Would she ever be able to put them behind her?

"This trailer is a mess." She put some room between them. "The police tore it up in their search."

"Are you certain it wasn't like this before this afternoon when they came inside?"

"George was the neatest man I ever met. Everything in its place." She couldn't help herself—she started straightening up the room. "I was in here right after I returned from Ireland and once again last week. If anyone else came in and made this mess, it would have to be in the last few days, which doesn't make sense."

She picked up mail tossed all over the table and gave each envelope a cursory go-over.

"What are you looking for?"

"I have no idea. I guess I'll know it when I see it."

But see it she didn't, not in what turned out to be mostly junk mail, everything from cable providers to retirement homes. Sure, like George had ever intended to retire. He said he'd work until the day he died. Now someone had made that wish come true, had retired him permanently. Her eyes stinging once more, she set down the mail and then replaced the two chairs that had been pulled out from the table.

Aidan helped her straighten up, at the same time examining the things that went through their hands—books, magazines, catalogs, souvenirs George had collected over the years. Everything was a mess, but nothing was out of place in that it didn't belong. And if anything was missing, she certainly couldn't tell.

Entering the bedroom, she stood before George's closet. "They went through everything in here, too." She picked up a couple of plaid shirts that had fallen to the bottom of the closet. "When I realized George had gone missing, I came in here, you know, just to check. There was a big empty spot in the center part of his closet where he'd removed clothes…um, if he really did."

"His clothing was gone?"

"It looked as though he'd packed up some things to take with him. And his small roll-around suitcase was missing. That's why the police thought he'd gone somewhere on impulse. He left the big suitcase and most of his clothes and personal items here. It's why I thought he would be back."

"But there was no suitcase buried with him."

That thought hadn't occurred to her. "No, there wasn't, but maybe—"

"We didn't miss it, Cat. The authorities checked

the area thoroughly but found nothing more or the detective would have told us."

"I wasn't even thinking about the suitcase when we talked to Pierce." She bent over to pick up a pair of pants and spotted what looked like a piece of cardboard kicked to the back of the closet, right next to a full-size suitcase. "Why wasn't the bag buried with George?"

"Maybe the killer still has it."

"So did George pack the bag himself or did the killer pack it for him?" Cat stooped to get the small item from the floor, thinking the smaller bag would have been stored there. "If George packed it, then he meant to leave. Maybe he was afraid of something and felt the need to get out of town. But if the killer packed it..."

"Then he would be trying to pull the wool over everyone's eyes. But would he really have reason to keep George's things?"

"I don't know." Cat's throat suddenly felt thick as she stood. "George could already have been dead. He could have been killed here somewhere on the property..." Staring at the cardboard she'd picked up from the closet floor, she frowned. "What the heck are these doing here?" She held up a book of matches to show him. "From Fernando's Hideaway. It's a bar just outside of town."

"Why are you so surprised?"

"George didn't smoke."

"Maybe he needed matches for something else—to light candles."

"But these are from a bar. George didn't go into bars. His father was an alcoholic and it ruined the family. George swore he would never take a drink himself."

"Perhaps he was with a friend. You can order a soft drink or coffee in a pub."

"You're probably right." Frowning, Cat slipped the matches into her jeans pocket. "Although he really was a loner." She thought a minute, then said, "We could check. It's less than ten minutes to Fernando's."

"'Tis been a long day, Cat."

"You don't have to go."

"You need a good night's sleep. We could go tomorrow night."

Realizing she wasn't fit to drive, Cat nodded. "You're right. I am exhausted." If only she *could* sleep. "I'm running on empty now."

"Then let's get you to bed."

Before she knew what he was about, Aidan took her in his arms. She stiffened—surely he wasn't going to make an advance on her here. But all he did was hug her and hold her for a moment until she relaxed against him. He felt so good. And leaning on him felt so right. She told herself not to be foolish. No more jumping off a cliff when it came to a man. Not like with Jack.

But Aidan wasn't like Jack, she reminded herself.

When he let go of her, she sighed, half in disappointment. It was best that nothing else happened between them, she thought. She let Aidan lead her toward the door. He insisted on driving back to the house, and she let him do that, as well.

Sinking into the passenger seat, she said, "Who could have killed him, Aidan? Who could have killed an elderly man who never did an unkind thing to anyone?"

"'Tis hard to know who holds a grudge against someone and why. Everyone has different sides to them. Your George could have made an enemy without you ever knowing."

"I must have been blind, then, because I never saw it. The people who worked for him respected him, even Bernie." Surely George riding the stable hand to get work done wasn't reason to kill him. "And the owners respected him, too. As a matter of fact, when my parents retired, Martin Bradley tried to hire him away from me—he has barns and a race-training facility a few miles from here. I know Martin offered him more money, but George was loyal to a fault. We might not have been blood, but he was family in every other way that counted."

Suddenly realizing they were parked in her drive, she opened the passenger door and stumbled out of the SUV. Within seconds, Aidan was at her side, steadying her and closing the door for her.

It felt so good to have a man willing to put himself out for her, a man who was honest and supportive.

If felt so good to be close to Aidan.

It would feel even better to be closer…

"Let's get you inside. You need to get to bed."

The dogs were waiting for the kitchen door to open. They greeted her with yips and madly wagging tails.

"Whist, now," Aidan said softly. "'Tis a hard day we have had."

Oddly enough, the dogs settled down immediately, though they shadowed Cat as Aidan walked her through the kitchen.

Part of her wanted to invite Aidan to join her just so she could feel a pair of strong arms around her. So she could feel not quite so alone.

Part of her wanted him to take her, drive the terrible images she still had from her mind.

Part of her wanted a redo, wanted to reset the clock to before she'd left for Ireland.

That was the problem, the reason for the guilt that was nagging her. If she hadn't ever left the farm for Ireland, George might still be alive. She couldn't stop thinking that it was somehow her fault that he'd been murdered.

Aidan stopped at her bedroom doorway where

he brushed his lips over her cheek. “Sleep well. Tomorrow will be a new day.”

Longing cut through her as she watched him go. The dogs pressed around her, now vying for her attention again. She absently patted them until the kitchen door closed behind Aidan.

Then she went into the bedroom and collapsed facedown on the bed.

HE STOOD FLATTENED against the side of the barn and watched the house with bated breath until the Irishman left it and took the stairs down to his quarters.

No police—they must not have found anything.

Safe for the moment.

That didn’t mean they were going to stop looking.

Another worry. He’d eaten a half-dozen antacids while they’d been in the barn manager’s trailer. Obviously they’d been searching through his things, looking for something that would tell them about the man’s death. He suspected not finding anything wouldn’t satisfy them. They’d keep poking around until they got into his business.

What next?

When could he stop looking over his shoulder?

His cell phone buzzed and he nearly jumped out of his skin.

Pulling it from his pocket, he fumbled with it, trying to answer before the noise alerted someone else.

One look at the name on the screen sent his stomach boiling again.

His hand shook as he lifted the cell phone to his ear. "What?"

"I heard they found George Odell's body in the ravine."

"So?"

"So, I was thinking that maybe George figured out what was going on and tried to stop you."

He did his best to keep his voice even. "I don't know what you're talking about."

"Sure you do. This is a whole different game."

"What do you want?"

"Motivation to stay silent."

More money—he knew it. "How much."

"A hundred thousand would do nicely."

He nearly choked on the amount, but he pulled himself together. "You'll have to give me a couple of days. I don't keep that kind of cash around."

"Two days."

Two days…was that enough time to eliminate another problem?

# *Chapter Eleven*

First thing the next morning, with Raul's help, Aidan loaded Mac into the trailer to take him to the track. If he'd dreamed the night before—whether of Cat or of murder—he wasn't aware of it. He hadn't heard stirrings above him, so he assumed Cat was still asleep. Good. She needed it after everything that had happened yesterday.

He couldn't help but think about their tryst in the forest preserve before finding her barn manager's body. What they'd done had been spontaneous and raw and exciting. And he couldn't help but want more.

But now, was that even possible? He'd sensed Cat's guilt after the discovery. And her longing last night. Which would win? Taking advantage of a woman in pain wasn't something he could do.

When they were on their way, Aidan turned his thoughts to the murdered barn manager. "My condolences, Raul."

"What for?"

"George Odell's untimely death. You worked with him every day. You must have been close."

"Yeah. Damn shame about him."

Raul sounded sincere, and Aidan noted his hands tightened on the steering wheel.

"Cat thinks he had no enemies."

"George was a good guy. Fair boss. Kept to himself mostly."

"So why would someone have reason to kill him?"

If Raul had a theory on that, he didn't say. He sank into silence. Aidan wished he knew the right questions to ask. Probably Raul knew him better than most people. Certainly in a different way than Cat.

Before he could figure out how to open the man up, get him to talk, Raul said, "Placido told me you don't want him to ride your horse."

"I never said that. First, it was a bad day to make important decisions. And then your brother jumped the gun, so to speak." He wasn't going to disparage the man to his brother for being so aggressive. Placido might indeed be the best jockey for the job, and he didn't want to cut out any possibilities yet. "I want to get Mac settled in his stall and out on the track first before I put him together with a jockey. The colt has a lot to say about who will ride him."

"You let the horse decide?"

"So to speak." He wasn't about to explain that he could sense whether or not there was a connection between a colt or filly and jockey.

"That's crazy, man, but whatever. You don't have no long time to think about it."

"I'm aware of that. I'll interview Placido in the next day or two."

"Yeah, if he's still available."

It occurred to Aidan that if Placido was the most winning jockey at the track, he should already have a ride. So what did the fact that he didn't have one mean? That he'd had an offer and lost the ride for some reason? Or that other owners and trainers were as put off by the man as he and Cat had been?

They pulled into the parking area behind the shedrow where Mac would be stabled, and as Aidan backed Mac out of the trailer, he ran his hands over the colt to soothe the tension out of his muscles. The colt relaxed only a little. He bobbed his head and sniffed the air of yet another new place. Though Mac was a good traveler, he'd done more of that than running since Aidan had decided to bring him to America. It was time he really got to stretch his legs.

"The tack room is at the end of the shedrow," he told Raul. "Just bring enough equipment to take Mac out on the track this morning. As soon as you're done, you can go back to the farm."

Raul simply grunted at him in response. Undoubtedly he was still out of sorts about his brother. Aidan led Mac to the shedrow. By the time they got to the stall, Nadim was coming toward them from the other direction.

"I just brought a horse back from a workout," the exercise rider said, giving Mac the once-over. "Hey, he's a real beauty. I have one more and then I have an hour before my next ride. I can work your colt if you want."

Grinning, Nadim reached up and gently ran a hand over Mac's nose. The colt blew into his palm and Aidan felt his tension ease up. Within seconds, Mac was snuffling Nadim's hair and then the front of his shirt. Laughing, Nadim pulled a piece of carrot from his pocket. The colt wasted no time in taking the offering.

"Grand. It seems Mac likes you, so you're in," Aidan said.

"Okay. See you right after I'm done."

Aidan was settling Mac into his new quarters when Raul delivered the tack and then quickly left for the farm. Aidan wondered how Cat was doing this morning?

He wished she could be here, not just to be part of Mac's first day, but because he missed her, as impossible as that seemed. They might have had sex, but they barely knew each other. And yet… in some way he felt as if they belonged together.

Foolish thought. Perhaps it was a fine thing that she had a mare in season, reason enough to keep them separated. He wondered that she could keep her mind on her job so soon after finding George.

And then there was Detective Pierce's promise to return. Had he already spoken to owners Dean Hill and Martin Bradley? Had he asked around town about George? If he'd learned something significant, would he share it with Cat?

Remembering his promise to check out Fernando's Hideaway with Cat this evening, he wondered what she hoped to learn. She wasn't some trained detective, but she was determined to help get justice for a man who was like family to her. He couldn't help but admire her for it.

Admiration was only one of the feelings he had for Catrina Clarke, Aidan thought. His blood stirred every time he was around her. He'd already felt her fire for the Thoroughbred business more than once. That alone made it hard to resist her, and when he simply thought of how much responsibility she shouldered alone without complaint, his heart stirred.

Something he didn't want to think too closely on. Something he didn't want to make real.

How could it be real in so short a time?

He simply needed someone in his life. He was tired of being lonely. And Cat just happened to be there, filling his head with what-ifs.

By the time he groomed the colt, picked and booted his hooves and tacked him up, Nadim had finished with his other ride.

It was early enough that there was still time to run him on the racetrack rather than the practice track, so after making certain Nadim could handle Mac, Aidan picked up a ride from another trainer driving in that direction. He was going to have to find time to rent some kind of vehicle long-term.

Aidan got to the track in time to see Nadim walk Mac halfway around to familiarize the colt with the sounds and smells and the feel of the dirt below his hooves. At the halfway mark, Mac was literally chomping at the bit to run, but Nadim kept in control, letting Mac trot, then extending the trot to stretch out Mac's muscles and get his blood circulating. Once he was properly warmed up, Nadim brought him to the fence to check with Aidan.

"He's good to go," said Nadim.

Indeed Mac was, and on Aidan's signal, go he did, finishing a mile and a quarter in two minutes two and a half seconds, about three seconds more than the Breeders' Cup Classic record. And this was just his first run on a real American track.

Aidan was pleased. And from the grin on Nadim's face, the exercise rider knew exactly what he had under him. In his element, Mac pranced and tried to get Nadim to let him run again, but the lad was strong enough to keep him in line.

"I have to get to the backstretch," Nadim said. "My next ride is in fifteen minutes."

"You can find a hotwalker?" Aidan asked. He would do it himself, but it looked like he was going to have walk back.

"No problem. There are plenty of guys hanging around, looking for more work."

Mac couldn't contain himself. The colt was making the exercise rider work to keep him in check. Following as best he could on foot, Aidan thought Nadim had possibilities as a jockey in the near future.

The distance between Aidan and his colt increased, and before he knew it, Mac disappeared behind the shedrow. It took Aidan another several minutes to catch up to them.

To his surprise, not only had Nadim removed the colt's tack, but he was handing Mac's lead to the stranger Aidan had seen watching him so intently the day before. On edge now, he told himself the lad had simply been looking for work. He couldn't shake the feeling that the young man looked familiar despite the billed cap and sunglasses that half-hid his face.

Realizing he'd caught up, Nadim said, "I need to get going to my next ride, Mr. McKenna. Tim here will cool Mac down."

"Thank you, Nadim. I shall see you tomorrow morning, then."

"Bright and early." Waving goodbye, Nadim jogged off down the shedrow.

Aidan turned to the hotwalker. "Tim, is it?"

"Tim Browne."

Aidan didn't miss the light lilt that reminded him of his homeland. So he'd been correct about recognizing him from somewhere. He watched Mac intently, put out his radar to make certain the colt was comfortable with the hotwalker. Everything seemed fine. More than fine.

Mac was pushing on the hotwalker like he knew him. Browne laughed and stroked the length of his nose.

Even so, when Browne moved off with Mac, Aidan kept pace with them.

"I'll walk with you a while, if you don't mind."

"'Tis your horse."

"Nothing personal. I simply like to make sure my horses are comfortable with the people who handle them."

Oddly enough, Mac was more than comfortable with someone who was a complete stranger. Browne kept his shoulder even with Mac's as they circled the shedrow. Just once, Mac tried to get ahead of him, but a sharp tug was enough to get the colt back where he belonged. Though the lad was nearly as small as Nadim, he was in control.

It took great strength to handle a twelve-hundred pound horse. Aidan didn't sense any resistance on Mac's part—the colt acted like the hotwalker was an old friend.

For some reason, that made Aidan even more uncomfortable.

"How long have you been working with the McHenry racehorses?" Aidan asked.

"I would be new here. Just as you are."

"And you are from Ireland. Just as I am."

"Aye."

"Some coincidence."

"Not at all. I sought you out. 'Tis grand to hear someone I can thoroughly understand."

Aidan could empathize with that. Though Americans spoke English, they all had different accents, and it took quite a bit of concentration to keep up with a conversation.

Browne let Mac take a short drink from a bucket attached to the end of the shedrow, checked his body temperature by placing his hand on Mac's chest, just below his neck. Mac snuffled his arm and looked at him expectantly.

"I think he wants you to give him a peppermint," Aidan said, pulling one from his pocket and handing it to the man.

"Here you go, then."

Mac lipped the peppermint from Tim's hand,

then swung his big head into the small man's shoulder.

Laughing, Browne reached up to scratch the sweet spot between the colt's ears and then continued walking him.

Amazed by the instant connection between horse and hotwalker, Aidan asked, "So what track did you work at in Ireland, Tim?" thinking that perhaps he and the colt had met previously.

"Ach, here and there. All over, really. I've actually been out of country the last few years."

Very nonspecific. "And here I was thinking we must have been at the same track at the same time before."

"Why is that?"

"I thought you looked familiar when I saw you yesterday."

Browne merely grunted and kept walking and watering the colt and checking his chest. Realizing he wasn't going to get more from the lad, Aidan simply went along for the walk, relying on his instincts. He simply didn't sense any reason to be suspicious of the hotwalker, no matter how much of a coincidence it was that they'd ended up at the same American track at the same time.

Browne repeated the process over and over until Mac was sufficiently cool. After rinsing the shedrow dirt from the colt's knees down in front, hocks down in back, Browne took Mac to his stall where he turned him loose.

"Do I qualify to work with your horse?" he asked Aidan.

"You'll do."

Standing at the stall opening, Aidan slipped another peppermint from his pocket and offered it to Mac. The colt lipped it into his mouth, bobbed his head and butted Aidan for attention. Aidan laughed and slipped his arms around the colt's neck. He ruffled his mane and in return, Mac snorted, chewed on his hair, then backed off and bobbed his head, as if saying *got you last*.

"You two seem to have a deeper connection than most."

"McKennas have a way with horses."

"So I've heard."

Browne saluted him and sauntered off, leaving Aidan to wonder what else the hotwalker had heard. He could understand him being drawn to work for another countryman, but how had he ended up at the same track? And why had Mac acted as if he already knew the man?

There was more to Tim Browne than met the eye.

Thinking he should find out what he could about the hotwalker, Aidan decided to call Cashel. After exchanging pleasantries and not such pleasant information about Cat's barn manager, Aidan got down to business.

"Mac ran ten furlongs this morning at the track. Two minutes, two and a half seconds."

"Not far from the record."

"And that a first attempt with an exercise rider on his back. A bit more training and a skilled jockey could narrow down the difference."

"Good lad. Give him a peppermint for me."

They spoke a few minutes about their hopes for the future. Then Aidan told Cashel about the hot-walker.

"Does the name Tim Browne ring a bell for you?"

"It does, but I can't place it," Cashel said. "Did he do something to raise your suspicions?"

"Not exactly. I think it was the way he was watching me yesterday. That raised my hackles. But he seems to be a skilled lad with the horses. And oddly enough, Mac acts like he already knows the man."

"Then I'll ask around. That makes it sound as if he's worked tracks here. Someone should know something about him."

"He said he's been out of Ireland. Whatever you learn, get back to me."

"That I shall." Cashel went silent for a moment, then said, "Aidan…I wish I could be there with you."

Aidan wouldn't lie—he was glad to be on his own for once—but he wouldn't hurt his brother's feelings. "Someone has to keep the business going. We can't let down our clients."

"If the colt makes it to the Classic, our clients here will have to do without me for a few days. I wouldn't miss that for the world."

Considering the Breeders' Cup was nearly six months away, Aidan figured he would be more than missing his autocratic older brother by then. "And I shall look forward to that day."

The conversation over, Aidan set off to find a groom and someone to muck Mac's stall twice a day, and found that Nadim had already set him up with candidates. And he should familiarize himself with the vets available at the track.

Mac's welfare only consumed half of him as he made for the midst of the backstretch.

The other part of his mind once again wandered to Cat and how she was doing, and he wished she could be here to share his good mood with him.

## *Chapter Twelve*

"Here I thought one or more of my client's broodmares would be in season today," Cat said, "and not only were they not in season, but Helen is certain Fairy Tail didn't conceive, so we'll have to try again."

"'Tis a shame," Aidan said, "but you need to believe that tomorrow will be better."

"I hope so. Things couldn't get worse. I spent most of the day making arrangements for George's burial. And I had to call my parents and brother and tell them. Mom broke into tears and immediately wanted to come up here for the service. I told her I was going to arrange a small gathering at the gravesite and thought she and Dad should wait until later, when they have plans to visit. We can do something to honor George then. That way, she'd have time to prepare what she wanted to do or say in his memory."

"Did she agree?"

"With Dad's influence." Cat swallowed hard.

"The police have already released George to the funeral director. I'll bury him two days after tomorrow. I'll put the word out for anyone who wants to come, but probably no one will even be there other than farm staff."

Aidan couldn't stand to see Cat so despondent. Perhaps he should be driving. Tension oozed from her. He recognized the connection that happened so seldom between him and another human being.

They were on their way to Fernando's Hideaway as they'd agreed the night before. There, they would not only see if anyone knew George but would get a bite to eat, as well. Looking forward to spending the evening in Cat's company, Aidan hoped to improve her mood.

He would give anything to see a real smile kiss her lips.

He would give anything to kiss them himself.

Shaking the temptation from his mind, he said, "Everything at the track is working out fine, at least. Nadim seems to be the perfect exercise rider. He arranged for a hotwalker, and later he sent over a groom. Good lad. Mac likes Nadim."

"And the hotwalker?"

"No problems there."

"There's something. I hear it in your voice."

Interesting that he couldn't fool her any more than she could fool him. "'Tis just that I thought I somehow should know the man. Tim Browne."

"Sorry, I don't recognize the name. Why did you think you should know him?"

"He looked familiar. He's another Irishman, and he's only been here a few weeks."

"So you're what? Suspicious of him?"

He echoed her sentiment. "There is something."

"So if you don't like him, hire someone else."

"I have no reason to dislike him, not on a feeling, not when Mac seems to really respond to him. He acts like he knows Browne, too. I simply don't believe in coincidence, so I called my brother and asked him about it. Cashel is familiar with the name but couldn't place him, either. He said that he would ask around. I'm probably worrying for naught."

"We have enough to worry about," Cat said as they pulled into town.

Not having seen Woodstock before, Aidan looked around with interest. Shops and restaurants in late nineteenth-century Victorian buildings and the historic Gothic revival–style Woodstock Opera House lined the streets around the square. In the center was a small park with a gazebo. A bunch of teenagers were hanging out there, while parents with small kids walked on an inner pathway.

Cat drove halfway around the square before taking a side street back out of town. "We're almost there. It's just a bit farther up the road."

"Perhaps while we're in town, you can show me where I can rent a vehicle. 'Tis too much of an inconvenience to you if your workers must play chauffeur for me."

"But there's no need to rent anything. At least not yet. I have a truck you can drive. It's old, but if you simply need a way to get back and forth to the track or to town, it'll do."

"Very kind of you. Are you certain you can spare a vehicle?"

"No one's using it anymore."

From her stiff tone, Aidan assumed the barn manager had been the one to use it in the past. He was thinking of how to respond when he saw the neon Fernando's Hideaway sign in front of a large one-story building with what looked like pale green siding in the fading light.

"Here we are." Cat pulled the SUV into the parking lot, which was already filling up.

A few minutes later, they were inside, being seated at a table halfway between the bar and the wall of windows that looked out on the parking lot. The hostess gave them menus and took their drink order. Aidan asked for a beer and, to his surprise, Cat did the same.

Opening his menu, he asked, "What is the specialty here?"

"Burgers are good," she said distractedly.

Aidan realized she was looking around the

room, he assumed for familiar faces. The tension she'd released in the SUV was back. He sensed her inner turmoil—the sensation was so strong, it was like a blow to him. He didn't normally read people. His brothers, yes. People he loved. So why Cat? And why was the connection so strong?

When the woman came back with the beers to take their food order, Cat asked, "Can you tell me if George Odell comes in here often?"

"Um, sorry, sweetie, don't know him. I've only been here a few weeks." The girl glanced over her shoulder. "The bartender Rob might know." And then, "Are you ready to order?"

They both ordered burgers and fries.

After the waitress left, Aidan said, "That didn't go as you wished."

"No, but there are plenty of people here to question. Starting with that bartender."

As they waited for their food, Aidan talked about Mac's training schedule, but he was aware that Cat was only half-listening, simply waiting to do what she'd come for. When they'd finished their burgers and fries, he insisted on paying and squared the check with the waitress. They then moved to a couple of empty seats at the bar.

"What can I get you?" the bartender named Rob asked.

Cat said, "Information."

"New drink?" he joked, raising a single dark eyebrow at her. "I hope you know what's in it."

"And I was hoping something, as well," Cat said. "George Odell used to come in here, right?"

"George Odell." The bartender's forehead pulled in a frown.

"Older man. Stocky. Thinning gray hair. A scar right here—" she pointed to the middle of her forehead "—where he got kicked by a horse."

"Sorry, doesn't sound familiar."

"You don't mind if I ask the other staff, do you?"

"This isn't my place, so you don't need my permission."

Rob waved his hand, indicating she should feel free. When Cat slid off her stool, he did the same.

"Stay here, have another beer," she said. "It'll only take me a few minutes."

"You heard the lass," Aidan told Rob, then looked back to Cat, who was approaching another waitress. "Whatever you have on draft will do."

The second waitress shook her head, so Cat went on to a busboy.

"Here you go," Rob said.

As Aidan turned to get his beer, the entry door opened, and to his surprise, who should walk in but Placido Ayala. So the jockey frequented this place? Maybe Cat should talk to him. But rather than taking a seat at a table or bar, Placido headed straight for the back and walked through a swinging door to what must be the kitchen.

Paying for the beer, he asked Rob, "So if you don't own this place, who does?"

"Fernando."

Wondering if that was a joke, he repeated, "Fernando?"

"Yeah, Fernando Ayala."

That perked up his inquisitive instincts. "Any relation to Placido or Raul?"

"Yeah, they're all brothers. There's another one, too. And a sister. They have a landscaping company down the road a piece."

Rob went to take care of another customer, and Aidan reached to the corner of the bar where he picked up a discarded pack of matches like the one found in George's closet.

"Well, that was a bust," Cat said, returning to the bar. She sounded choked, but as if she was trying not show it. "No one seems to have ever seen George in here. They didn't even know who he was."

"Your barn manager may never have been in here, after all," Aidan said.

Seeing what he was holding in his hand, she asked, "Then where did the matches come from?"

Aidan told her about Raul being related to the owner.

The nagging feeling of spinning out of control would be finished tonight. He was counting on it. He was ready to do what was necessary.

The hour to meet was here, the air was still, the moon was under cloud cover.

He would be invisible.

Popping an antacid in his mouth, he chewed fast and waited until he swallowed before getting out of the vehicle, case in hand, checking his pocket before walking to the back door of the appointed place.

He knocked and swallowed hard, counting the seconds that ticked by.

When the door opened, he nodded and entered, passing his accomplice without speaking.

"You have the money?"

He held out the case, and as it exchanged hands he said, "This will be it. No more."

"Not a good attitude. We're partners in this, after all."

The spite-filled statement made him see red. He'd done all the damn work, had taken all the risks! As the case opened, and greedy fingers picked up one stack of bills and then the other, he slipped the syringe from his pocket and removed the tip.

"What the hell? A case full of tens? This isn't a hundred thousand!"

"Doesn't matter what it is." From behind, he

jammed the needle through clothing into flesh and pressed the plunger to release the contents before his victim could turn to fight. "You won't get to spend any of it anyway."

Then he stepped out of the way of grasping hands and watched as his liability became ineffective, eyes bulging at him, throat scraping out ineffectual sounds. A minute, and his amusement ended.

He stepped over the body and opened a cabinet to find what he needed, and realized something of great importance.

The first murder had nearly finished him.

Now he felt almost refreshed knowing that there was one less obstacle standing in his way.

The second time had been easier.

He could do whatever was necessary.

HER MIND WHIRLING, Cat let Aidan drive.

"So if George never went to Fernando's," she said, "someone could have given them to him. Or dropped them while taking the suitcase out of the closet." Her pulse drummed because she didn't want to believe it. "Of course that's most likely Raul, right?"

"I would not venture to guess. I asked him about George and he seemed to be sincere that he was sorry about the man's death."

Aidan had such good instincts, Cat wanted to

trust them. Wanted to trust Raul, who had worked for her since she took over the business. George had been the one to hire and train him. They might not have been buddies, but they'd always seemed to get along.

"Placido, then?" she mused. "What would he be doing at the farm?"

"He never came onto your property to visit his brother?"

"Yeah, sure, a few times. That's how I met him, though I don't remember seeing him around lately."

"Maybe because he's had reason to avoid the farm."

Though she didn't much like Placido, Cat hated thinking anyone she knew was involved in George's death. But it only made sense. Her barn manager might not have been buried on her property, but it wasn't much of a stretch to believe he'd been taken from the farm to the forest preserve, where he'd been dumped in the ravine.

When Aidan turned through the farm gates, she viewed the property with mixed feelings. All her life, this had been her home, her shelter, her safe place. But if George had been killed here, how safe could the farm really be?

A shiver set through her to her very core. Every movement and every shadow seemed to hold some secret menace.

She didn't want to be alone.

So when they got out of the SUV and approached the house, Cat said, "Why don't you come in for a minute? I'll get you the keys to the truck." If only she could get him to stay for a while, until she settled down inside.

"It's late. I can fetch them in the morning."

"No!" Flushing at her intense reaction, Cat tried for a logical explanation. "I mean, you might be up before me and want to leave for the track. I don't want you to have to wait around until I wake up."

"All right, then."

As she unlocked the back door, Aidan was right behind her, so close she could almost feel him pressed to her backside. Tempted to stop and lean back against him, she forced herself inside. As usual, the dogs were waiting for her. She stopped for a moment to pet them and give them treats, then sent them to their run and locked them out of the house so they wouldn't pester her for a while.

"The keys are in the living room. It's the old, rusty black truck parked behind the barn."

She headed through the kitchen and went straight for the desk nestled below the bay window. The keys were in the top drawer. Not wanting to be alone, wishing for Aidan's company, she turned to him, hand extended, keys dangling from her forefinger.

"Here. Before you leave, can I offer you a drink?"

"'Tis not a drink I need."

He reached for the keys and their hands touched and they both froze. The increased pulse in her throat startled her.

"Tea?" she choked out.

"Not thirsty."

He moved a bit closer. His voice cut through her and his heat teased her and she could think of only one thing.

"What, then?" she asked softly. "What is it you need?"

"This."

His arms wound around her back and he pulled her closer. Her breath caught in her throat as she waited for his lips to touch hers. It took forever, as if he were giving her a chance to push him away.

As if he thought she might not want this.

Sliding her hands up his chest, she lightly grasped his shoulders, feeling like she needed to hold on to him to stay upright. And maybe she did. Her pulse thrummed and sped up when his mouth covered hers.

The kiss was soft and sweet and filled with longing.

Or maybe that was her.

She longed for a man who would partner her. A man she could count on. One who would spice up her life with the wild and exciting and unexpected. Someone who could heal her wounded heart.

A flash of the dogs digging up George suddenly sent ice water through her veins.

As if he read her shift in mood, Aidan whispered, “I apologize” against her lips.

“No. I wanted you to kiss me. I want…more.”

She needed more, to chase away the horrid images in her mind. To chase away the fear. To feel safe in his arms.

This time, she kissed him and slid her hands to his belt and unbuckled it.

Aidan groaned when she touched him. He came alive in her hand. Dropping to her knees, she explored him with her mouth until he fell back against the desk. He wound shaking hands through her hair and pushed against her mouth as she tasted him. Then he pulled her back up to her feet and kissed her again while undressing her. She let him do what he would, losing herself in every touch…touching and stripping him in return.

Finally, when they were both naked, Aidan bent her backward and followed over her, dropping them both gently down to the floor. As he entered her, Cat wrapped her legs around his hips and rolled, landing on top. Riding him, she lost herself in every touch, every movement.

For now, at least, their tangled bodies were enough to chase away the nightmare her life had become.

SHE WAS IN THE BARN IN *the dark again, checking on the broodmares.*

*Wind soughed between the timbers and she stopped to listen. Dread filled her but she continued working, hurrying to finish, all the while knowing she wasn't alone.*

*She raced to leave the barn, but the shadowy figure caught up to her.*

*A sharp pain in her back stopped her. Paralyzed her. Though she tried, she couldn't move.*

*Couldn't avoid what was coming...*

Aidan awoke with a gasp and quickly oriented himself. He was in bed with Cat. She was there next to him.

Asleep.

Safe.

For how long?

What did the dream mean? That she would be attacked and drugged? But why?

Should he warn her?

No, of course not. He'd learned not to trust his dreams. Learned that he had to sort truth from fantasy.

That was the trouble with his ability. Dreams held only half-truths, hid the rest.

So what was the nugget of truth in this one?

He would be on alert for any further sign of trouble. But on thinking about it, Aidan considered he might have mixed his growing feelings for Cat with the horrific scene they'd encountered in the woods.

Strong emotions could distort dreams into nightmares.

Next to him, Cat turned in her sleep and made a sound of discontent.

Aidan immediately settled back in and wrapped himself protectively around her.

## *Chapter Thirteen*

Both Diamond Dame and Sweetpea Sue were in season. Finally! Though Cat was certain of it, she wanted Helen to check them out before proceeding. Having slept in fits and starts once she'd landed in her bed with Aidan, she didn't trust her own judgment. The trouble was, the vet hadn't shown up to check out Fairy Tail as she'd said she would.

Cat placed a call but got Helen's voice mail, so she left a message. Then she called both Martin Bradley and Dean Hill to tell them their mares were in season. More voice mails. More messages.

After waiting to hear from someone for nearly an hour, her nerves were on edge. She called the vet again and had to leave yet another message.

"Hi, Helen. Cat. Just trying to scare you up. I'm waiting for you to check on the mares who are finally in season. And on Fairy Tail. Call even if you can't make it, okay?"

Hanging up, she shoved the cell phone back in her pocket.

What now?

Raul came up from behind her, asking, "Do you want to get started?"

She didn't want to, not really. She wanted a day off. Maybe a week off. How long did it take to get over deep grief? But she was running a business and she had two broodmares who were going to help pay her bills, and she couldn't ignore that. It didn't mean she'd loved George any less or that she would forget him. That was part of the problem. She couldn't erase the picture of the dogs digging him up from her mind.

Or what she and Aidan had been doing just before the dogs found him.

"The mares?" Raul reminded her.

"Since we have two ready for cover, I guess we really can't wait any longer." The owners would expect her to breed their mares, vet or no vet. "I don't understand why Helen isn't getting back to me. She was supposed to be here this morning and didn't even call to tell me that she was going to be late."

Raul didn't comment on the vet's disappearing act. Instead, he asked, "Which mare do we cover first?"

Martin Bradley chose that moment to walk in on them.

"My mare first," he demanded. "Hill's not here, so his mare can wait. Two of his are already pregnant anyway."

Not that it mattered, Cat thought. Getting to both of them in the same day would be no problem. Neither was going to go out of season in one day. Still tense after all that had happened the day before, she didn't need any added pressure.

Thankfully, Dean Hill hadn't gotten back to her, so she nodded and said, "Have Bernie bring out Sweetpea Sue, and you handle On the List."

"If she's ready, she doesn't need a teaser stallion." Martin pushed a tense hand through his dyed hair. "Just bring out Desert Son and let him mount her and get it over with. I want it done."

What in the world was wrong with him? Cat wondered. She'd been working with Martin for several years now, and normally he let her do her job with little involvement. Something was going on with him, though, and she didn't want to make things worse.

"Okay, Raul. Desert Son it is."

Undoubtedly Martin was competing with Dean Hill, the only reason she could think of for him to sound so…so desperate. He'd always been demanding, but he'd also been professional and had let her do her job without interference. While two of Dean's mares were already pregnant this early in the breeding season, Martin had already expressed his displeasure that his own mares hadn't yet taken.

Cat could only hope Sweetpea Sue would break the unlucky streak.

Thankfully, both Raul and Bernie had a good hand with the horses, and under Cat's guidance, getting the horses ready for breeding went smoothly. Desert Son required no assistance, and the cover was quick.

But before the horses were even settled enough to take back to their stalls, Dean Hill stormed into the back of the barn where they were working.

"What is this? Where is Diamond Dame?"

Starting at the anger in his voice, Cat said, "She's in her stall."

"So you've already finished with her?"

"No, Dean," Cat said, "we haven't started her cover yet."

"What are you waiting for?"

"In case you're blind," Martin Bradley said, "my Sweetpea, who is also in season, was just covered by my stallion."

"So Bradley has precedence?" Dean demanded to know.

Before Cat could answer, Martin did it for her. "Why should you have precedence, Hill? You weren't even here. My mares haven't been as fruitful as yours. Besides, I should have priority. I've been Cat's client since she took over the business!

And I was her father's client before that. You're new to this barn."

"This barn is lucky to have me!"

Openmouthed at the argument, worried the men would come to physical blows, Cat signaled her workers to take the mare and stallion back to their stalls. "You'll both be taken care of properly, just as I take care of all my clients. I don't understand the problem, Dean."

"The problem? What's the problem? No sooner have I committed my broodmares to your care than I'm questioned by Wade Pierce concerning the murder of one of your employees! And now this."

George's death came crashing back on Cat. She'd feared the owners might be upset by being involved in the investigation, but there was no helping it.

"Did you do it, Hill?"

Martin's accusatory tone made Cat's heart skip a beat.

Dean yelled, "Are you crazy?"

"Let's all calm down, please," Cat said.

"Right. It's not *Cat's* fault that George was murdered." Martin narrowed his gaze on her. "It's not, is it?"

"What!" Cat felt the need to hold on to a nearby post to keep herself upright. Maybe she should have taken that day off.

"Cat wasn't even in the country when George disappeared, you numbskull!" Dean took a big breath. "All right. I'm calm. And I apologize for being out of line. I couldn't get here when you called, Cat, because Pierce caught me before I could leave my place. He just got under my skin, is all. I shouldn't take it out on you." He looked to Martin. "Didn't Pierce question you?"

"Yesterday evening. He has to question everyone, Hill. I didn't like it any better than you did. I've just had more time to process it."

"Detective Pierce can only get to you if you let him," Cat said, hoping to calm the men so they could get back to business. "He's been questioning everyone who worked with or knew George. Even the kids who muck out the stalls."

Even Aidan, who hadn't yet left his home in Ireland when George had disappeared.

Cat wished Aidan was here now. She would guess he was good at dealing with irate horse owners. He'd been good at keeping her on an even keel the day before. His strength would be welcome. He would be welcome. She was having more and more trouble keeping Aidan from her thoughts.

"I know Pierce wasn't targeting us," Dean said, sounding a bit more calm.

"But it sure felt like he was," Martin admitted.

"All right." Dean held out his hand to the other man. "I apologize if I was an ass."

Martin took his hand and shook on it before leaving.

Crisis averted, Cat got back to work. Satisfied that Sweetpea Sue might be on her way to conceiving, she instructed Raul and Bernie to get Diamond Dame and False Promise ready for cover.

On the surface, she remained calm, breeding Dean's mare as professionally as she always did. The owner—his charming self once more—apologized to her again and thanked her for doing such a great job for him. Cat smiled through it all, but underneath, worry—and guilt—ate at her.

If the adults had been so traumatized by the police investigation, what about the poor kids who had actually worked for George five days a week?

So when Laura and Vincent arrived after school, Cat was relieved that they seemed…well, like normal teenagers.

"Where do you want to start?" Vincent asked his companion as they entered the barn together.

"How about I muck and you haul?"

"Hey, I thought this was an equal-opportunity job."

Laura sighed. "It's just that the wheelbarrows are so big and you're so *strong,* Vincent. But, okay. Maybe I just won't completely fill it. Then it won't be so heavy," the girl said dramatically.

"All right, all right. I'll haul your old wheelbarrow."

Cat smothered a grin and realized this felt like the first natural moment she'd experienced since she and Aidan had followed the dogs into the ravine. Thankful that the kids seemed unaffected by the police investigation, she moved toward them and pretended she'd just realized they'd arrived.

"Oh, there you two are."

"We're on time," Laura said anxiously.

"And ready to work hard," Vincent added.

"Well, good. But before you start, I wonder if you've seen something around here somewhere."

"What?" they asked in unison.

"A suitcase. You know one of those small cases with wheels…silvery-gray…the kind you take on a plane with you."

"You brought it in the barn?"

"Not me. George did," Cat said, noting the immediate shift in tension. Laura's expression fell, and Vincent stepped closer to her and wrapped an arm around her shoulders as he'd done before. "Well he may have brought it in here," Cat explained. "Whatever, it's missing and if we found it, maybe there could be some kind of clue that would help the authorities figure out what happened…" She let her words trail off. "So, you haven't seen it?"

"Not me," Vincent said.

Avoiding Cat's eyes, Laura simply shook her head.

It had been a long shot, but one worth taking. "Well, thanks. Just keep an eye open for it."

"Sure." Vincent looked at Laura, his features pulled in concern. "You okay?"

"Fine." Laura pulled away from him as if to prove it. "Let's get started."

Maybe the girl wasn't so fine, after all, Cat thought, but she was putting up a good front. Both kids were so responsible. Just like she had been at that age.

Cat realized she hadn't had anything but coffee and a piece of toast that morning. She headed for the house. The dogs shot out of nowhere to join her.

Now if only Aidan were here, she thought wistfully.

How had he become so important to her in so short a time?

AIDAN WAS RIDING ON AIR. Mac had shaved a half second off his ten-furlong time this morning. The vet he'd chosen to take care of the colt at the track had looked Mac over and declared him to be in top shape. His team on the backstretch was set but for the jockey. Placido had come by again, but Aidan was wary of hiring him.

Personally, his relationship with Cat made him feel emotional stirrings that he'd thought had been buried. Perhaps he could have another chance at happiness, after all.

And then, before Aidan could say goodbye to Mac and leave for the farm, Cashel called.

"I did some digging on Browne."

A shudder of anticipation shot down Aidan's spine. "And what might you have learned?"

"Your hotwalker is not a hotwalker."

Mac poked his nose at his owner for attention. Aidan patted him absently and left the stall, saying, "I don't understand."

"Tim Browne is a jockey."

Aidan started. The man was the right size. He was still working around horses and obviously very good with them. So why wasn't he riding them? "He must be a poor jockey if we weren't able to place the name."

"Just the opposite, though he wasn't riding in Ireland."

Aidan moved down the shedrow. "He said he'd been out of country. Where, then? Not in America, was he? He's only been here a few weeks. No, wait. He said he's only been at McHenry a few weeks."

"Not America," Cashel said. "Australia. He was part of the Irish team asked over there for the Ireland vs. Australia Jockey competition."

Aidan knew the six-event challenge concluded with Irish Day, the second largest race meeting in South Australia every year. Being part of the team was prestigious.

"Then why didn't we know his name?" Aidan stopped at the end of the shedrow before going on to his loaner truck.

"Because that was seven years ago. He liked the change of scenery and decided to settle there for a while."

"Seven years. He must have loved it. Or someone," Aidan added, thinking how he'd miss Cat if he had to return to Ireland.

"I don't know about his love life," Cashel said. "What I do know is that more than a year ago, a horse broke down under him in a big race. Browne had several broken bones himself. He spent months going through surgery and rehabilitation. He returned to Ireland a few months ago and never even raced while he was here."

"And then decided to change countries again?" Aidan shook his head. That didn't make sense. Not unless Browne had made the move for some other purpose. Making certain no one was around to hear, he said, "I still think it an odd coincidence that we both landed here in Woodstock, Illinois, in the middle of the United States at nearly the same time."

"Aye," Cashel agreed. "'Tis an odd thing."

A thing that sent suspicion skittering through Aidan.

Tim Browne had arrived at McHenry Racecourse not long before him but after Cat had made her partnership offer. It was almost as if the man had been tracking his movements and arranged the coincidence of meeting him here. So he could hotwalk Mac? Or so that he could race him? If so, why hadn't Browne approached him the way Placido had? Why would a jockey pretend he was something other than a jockey?

# *Chapter Fourteen*

Their sharing a bed seemed inevitable. At the end of another difficult day, the only thought that made Cat feel better was not being alone. When Aidan took her in his arms, she sensed his need, as well. He held her close. Protectively. And something inside her blossomed.

Things were getting scary between them.

It wasn't just the sex anymore.

While she enjoyed every minute together, every kiss, every touch, Cat looked forward to what came afterward, to being held in strong arms that made her feel like she wasn't alone.

Like she was safe.

With her head tucked against his chest, the drum of Aidan's heartbeat lulled her to sleep.

Waking sometime later, she regretted having to leave his side. He didn't so much as stir as she pulled away from him, slipped out of bed and pulled on some clothes.

She needed to check on the two mares she'd bred that day.

Topaz and Smokey dogged her through the kitchen. She ruffled their ears and left them behind.

The night was dark, the wind blowing in gusts as it had two nights ago. No sign of rain, though, something for which she was grateful. She didn't need to be spooked again—over the past few days, she'd experienced enough fear for a lifetime.

As was her habit, when she entered the barn, she felt for the flashlight on its wall hook. A soft nicker from one direction and a hoof meeting a barn board from another froze her in place.

The wind soughed between the timbers.

Her heart kicked up a beat and she held her breath to listen. When she didn't hear anything more, she grabbed the flashlight, and, clicking it on, gave a cursory sweep of the barn. The only thing she accomplished was to disturb several horses who grumbled at her.

Thinking that since she'd bred Sweetpea Sue first she should check on her first, Cat turned toward the aisle where Martin's horses were stabled. Something didn't feel right, but she put it to nerves. And yet…a few steps more and she swore she heard a noise behind her.

"Who's there?" she cried, turning smack into a wall of pain.

The inside of her head lit up like a fireworks display.

And then flickered out.

AIDAN LUNGED OUT OF A dreamless sleep to find Cat's side of the bed empty and both dogs barking like they were desperate to get out of the house.

Heart thundering, he called, "Cat?" and when she didn't answer, tore out of bed and into his jeans.

The dogs came to his call. They barked at him now, their voices tinged with anger and fear. Focusing on the sound, connecting with the dogs the same way he had when they'd gone down into the ravine, he fine-tuned what they were trying to tell him.

Cat was in trouble.

No…not the nightmare come true!

He hadn't warned her…

Shoving his feet into his boots, he grabbed his T-shirt and pulled it over his head as he rushed out of the bedroom. The dogs were ahead of him, waiting with growls at the back door even as he took his first step into the kitchen.

The horses…she must have gone out to the barn to check on them.

When Aidan opened the back door, the dogs exploded outward with him. There was no keeping them back. They raced to the barn. Just inside, they stopped and began whining.

Dear Lord, he hoped Cat was all right.

Running, he got to the entry in seconds and felt for the light switches. The barn lit up. The horses squealed and snorted. And the dogs stood guard on either side of Cat, who was sprawled facedown on the barn floor.

It hit Aidan like a hammer—the knowledge that he'd done this, that Cat being hurt, or worse, was his fault.

He'd dreamt it and he hadn't warned her, hadn't forbidden her from coming into the barn alone at night.

Not that she would have believed him any more than Pegeen had.

Sheelin O'Keefe had struck again, straight from her grave, and he'd let it happen. He only hoped he wasn't too late to save another woman who'd captured his heart.

"Oohh."

To his relief, Cat stirred, and the dogs whined and stuck their noses in her hair and Aidan dropped to his knees beside her.

"What happened?" she croaked, rolling over.

He helped her sit and cupped her chin. Gently, he turned her head so he could take a better look. Blood oozed from a cut on her forehead that slashed into her hairline. His chest tightened, for he was reminded of finding George with his head bashed in. But this veered off from what he'd seen in his sleep the night before.

"It looks as if someone wanted you unconscious."

She tried to put a hand to the cut, but he grabbed her wrist to stop her.

"Do not touch the wound, or you will surely put yourself in a world of pain. Do you remember anything?"

She frowned and thought a moment. "I came to check on Sweetpea Sue and Diamond Dame. I had just gotten the flashlight when I thought I heard something. I turned and…I guess someone clobbered me."

Aidan immediately wanted to find whoever had done this to her and give him some of his own medicine. But whoever was probably long gone. And Cat was his first concern.

"Are you hurt anywhere else?" Had someone shot her up with something?

"No. Would you move so I can get up?"

"And your head is clear?"

"As much as it can be, considering I got hit pretty hard."

So she wasn't drugged. Where had that part of the dream come from?

He said, "I just wanted to make certain it was all right to let you up."

She frowned at him then. “I can get up myself.”

Before she could try, he hooked hands under her arms and practically lifted her to her feet. The dogs crowded them, expressing their concern in low, pitiful voices.

“She is all right now,” Aidan told them. Intent on easing their distress, he patted each dog reassuringly and silently communicated—*Calm down...your mistress will be fine*—even if he didn’t quite believe it himself.

A noise issued from the rear of the barn, and both dogs went back on alert.

Aidan turned to see Bernie coming toward them.

“What the heck happened?” he demanded.

“Bernie, what are you doing here at this time of night?” Cat asked.

“I heard the commotion the dogs were making all the way back in my trailer. I came to see what was wrong. Are you okay?”

She groaned. “I’ll live.”

She would for the moment…but for how long? Aidan wondered, realizing how deep his feelings for Cat went. Surely he couldn’t lose a second woman to Sheelin’s curse.

Hoping that Bernie hadn’t had anything to do with the attack, he said, “I need to get Cat to the nearest emergency room.” Fearing she wouldn’t be able to give him directions to the hospital in her condition, he asked Bernie for that information. Then he said, “Would you look around, make certain there is no one here on the property who doesn’t belong?”

“Yeah, sure.”

“And check on the mares,” Cat added. “I never got a chance.” As Aidan headed her straight for the SUV, she stopped. “I don’t really need to see a doctor. A couple of aspirins and an ice bag will do.”

Not willing to let her beg off, Aidan lifted her into his arms and kept going toward the vehicle. She didn’t fight him, merely lay flaccid against his chest, her head tucked under his chin. His pulse was racing and his gut was in knots, and a dread he’d only once before experienced filled him. He steeled himself against showing what he was feeling.

“I beg to differ about the doctor, Cat. You could have a concussion. I will not be taking that chance.” He stopped at the SUV and set her on her feet. When he opened the passenger door for her and helped her into the seat, he realized the dogs were there, waiting for an invitation to get in. “Sorry, you cannot come,” he said, and closed the door.

The dogs sat and watched with sorrowful eyes as he rounded the vehicle, got behind the wheel and fetched Cat’s keys from where she kept them in a compartment above his head. Starting the car, he glanced at her and realized how shaken she appeared to be.

"How bad is the pain?"

"Bearable. I just want to close my eyes and go back to sleep."

"No sleeping until you have been checked over."

Once on the road, he pulled out his cell phone and called the authorities, who promised to send someone to the E.R. to take a report, as well as to the farm to investigate the scene of the crime.

"Talk to me and keep talking," he urged Cat.

"About what?"

"Anything. I just need to know that you are all right. Tell me about your horses."

Cat did as he asked. "Dangerous Illusion—that's my stallion—" she reminded him "—was born on the farm. Dad bred his sire and dam and foaled him for Martin Bradley, who raced him as a two-year-old and as a three-year-old. Dangerous Illusion was fast, but despite his lineage he wasn't a champion. He won a few Grade 2 and Grade 3 races, but he never made the big time. He was difficult, too. Temperamental. He can be impossible at times. But when he cooperates, he makes beautiful foals."

"So your father bought him from Bradley?"

"Actually, I did when I took over the business."

Aidan only listened with half an ear. His attention wandered to Pegeen and how she'd died because he'd thrown caution to the wind and had defied the curse and he hadn't done what was necessary to stop her. As a result, he'd put her in mortal danger and had lost her. He'd thought the curse was over, had even thought he might be able to find happiness again. At the moment, his emotions were in overdrive, proof that he'd been unable to keep himself from becoming overly attached to Cat.

Apparently, he was falling in love with her.

Apparently, the curse wasn't over.

The moment he'd allowed himself to hope there was some happiness in his future, it was taken from him.

But did it have to be this time?

He had to tell Cat about the curse and about the warning in his dreams, but would she believe him any more than Pegeen had? Remembering how close-minded she'd been about his psychic connection with Mac, Aidan wasn't certain that she would. She'd compared him to her ex-husband, who'd lied to her and had betrayed her. Would she think the same of him, that he was lying to get close to her?

Still, he had to find some way to tell her. To warn her. To make her believe him when he told her that her life could be in danger.

And if he couldn't convince her, what then?

# *Chapter Fifteen*

By the time Cat was released from the hospital, it was midmorning the next day. The doctor had insisted on keeping her overnight for observation. After making out a report with the uniformed officer who had come to the hospital, she'd slept only to be awakened once an hour to make sure she didn't have a concussion. And Aidan had spent the night in a semicomfortable-looking chair.

He looked absolutely haggard.

"I'm sorry you missed Mac's morning workout."

"It couldn't be helped. Nadim took Mac out on the track. His time was a bit off yesterday, but only by less than two seconds."

*Not good,* Cat thought, but she didn't care to point that out to a man who was probably worried already. She didn't need to add to his burden. He should have gone to the racetrack for the morning workout and come back for her.

"You can still go out there after you let me off—"

"Nah, nah, I will not be doing that until I am sure you are safe." He hesitated a moment and added, "Your life may be in danger."

How he could be confident of any such thing, she wasn't certain. Still, she had to remain positive. She wouldn't live in fear.

"It was a random event, Aidan, probably a thief just looking for something he could take and hock and I interrupted him." She had to believe that. The alternative—that it was someone she knew—was unthinkable. "I won't go out to the barn alone at night anymore."

"The authorities did not find any indication of mischief or theft."

"Maybe my walking in on him was enough to scare the intruder away."

"I would like to think that."

"What *do* you think?"

"That I'm to blame."

Cat started. "You? Why would you say that?"

"'Tis the McKennas' lot to lose the people they care about."

He cared about her? Her pulse quickened. "I don't understand."

"'Tis a curse."

She listened to his story about Sheelin O'Keefe and Donal McKenna, and how when Donal left the supposed witch for another woman, Sheelin cursed his progeny to put their loved ones in mortal danger.

"You certainly have an open mind," Cat said. "You believe in a psychic connection with your horses. And now a witch's curse."

"You think I am making all this up?" He sounded upset.

"I think you have an Irish sense of whimsy."

"Is that what it is?"

"It makes a good story."

"'Tis all true!" Aidan argued. "My family has lost too many loved ones to think otherwise."

"Everyone loses someone they care about."

"But not always the person who is their soul mate."

Was there such a thing? "Your mother is still alive, isn't she?"

"Aye, but she wasn't my da's true love. He let the woman who has his heart go rather than bring Sheelin's curse on her head."

Cat frowned. "Did your mother know this when she married him?"

"That she did, indeed. She loved Da, and Da treats her with the greatest respect. 'Tis only occasionally the melancholy sets in him and he drinks to forget."

"But no one died."

"Not that time, because Da avoided the curse."

What other time was he referring to? she wondered. "What a sad life your father must lead believing in curses and therefore never accepting love." And how sad that Aidan was following in his footsteps.

"So you refuse to believe me."

Cat realized he sounded angry and upset that she didn't. As incredible as this curse thing sounded, she could sense he really did believe in it.

"No offense, Aidan. I'm not sure my sense of whimsy was ever that advanced. Or if it was, Jack killed it for me."

Aidan made a strangled sound. "Perhaps you need to open your mind. Many things in the world have no logical explanation."

What wasn't he saying? "I'm just not there. I'm sorry, Aidan, but none of this makes sense to me. I simply don't believe it. If you're letting this supposed curse rule your life, then I feel sorry for you."

"'Tis you that gives me worry."

"Stop worrying, please. I'm fine."

He'd said something about caring. Was that why he was so worried about her? Was that why he was telling her all this? Did he think he was in love with her?

Her heart nearly stopped at the thought.

Surely not. They barely knew each other. And yet…

She knew Aidan well enough to realize that he was a man of honor, one whose feelings ran deep, one who worked hard and dreamed big. They came from the same world of Thoroughbred horses, and that world was their life. They had more in common than not.

Aidan McKenna was exactly the kind of man she'd always hoped to have in her life.

Burned by the emotionally destructive relationship with her ex-husband, having thought she would never be attracted to another horseman, Cat had complex feelings about Aidan.

Jack was a liar and a cheat.

Aidan was a man she could count on.

Who else but another horseman—an honorable one—would understand her, share in her triumphs, support her when things went wrong?

Thinking about it—examining her own feelings—was too much for Cat right now, so she tucked the disturbing thoughts away. At some later date, she would take them out and analyze them.

Just not now.

As the SUV turned onto farm property, Cat realized they had company. A police car sat in front of the house, and Detective Wade Pierce leaned on the hood waiting for them. Aidan pulled up next to the police car, then hopped out and rushed around to the passenger door to help Cat out. Though she was still moving slowly and her head throbbed if she turned it too fast, she was feeling better than she had even a few hours ago. She walked toward Pierce, Aidan supporting her with an arm around her back that felt really good. And right.

"Detective Pierce, I'm surprised to see you here."

"I called the hospital and they told me you'd been released, so I figured I might as well come straight to the farm."

"I didn't know you worked attempted burglaries."

"I don't. Can we go inside? You're not looking too good. You probably need to sit down."

That didn't make Cat happy. Why did she need to sit? Had he found out something definitive about George's murder and was reluctant to tell her?

She let Aidan lead her inside. "The dogs aren't here."

"I called earlier. Bernie said he would feed them. They have probably followed him, wherever he is."

Sitting, she asked, "So what is it, Detective? You learned something about George?"

"Afraid not. I have more bad news. This time it's about Helen Fox."

"The veterinarian?" Aidan asked.

"Yes." Cat could hardly catch her breath. "What happened?"

"I'm afraid she's dead."

Cat gasped and Aidan clasped her shoulder to let her know he was there to support her.

"The cleaning woman found her body this morning, but we think she was murdered about thirty-six hours ago."

"Murdered?" Cat could hardly fathom it. First George, now Helen. She'd never known another person who'd been murdered and here there were two people she'd known well in the space of a month. "No wonder I couldn't scare her up yesterday. I called several times."

"Yes, we know. We found her cell phone and ran through all her messages."

"What happened?" Aidan asked.

"The paramedics who brought her in thought she'd had a heart attack—"

"But she's only in her early forties!" Cat said.

"Which is why the ME performed an autopsy. There was one needle mark in her back and another in her neck. It seems that she was sedated and then injected with a second drug intravenously."

Cat cried out. “Are you saying she was euthanized like a horse?”

“Exactly like she would have put down a horse or any other animal. The drugs were right there in her office.”

“Oh, no,” Cat whispered.

“’Tis a terrible thing,” Aidan said. “Do you have any idea of who the murderer might be?”

“Obviously someone familiar with animals and the drugs and method used to euthanize them. Possibly the same person who killed George Odell.”

“They were not killed in the same way, so how do you make that connection?” Aidan asked.

“They have something in common. This farm.” He locked gazes with Cat. “And you. All three incidents in less than a month.”

Cat’s pulse leaped, and Aidan seemed to sense it. He moved in closer so she could feel him and put his hands over her shoulders.

She tried to catch her breath. “I—I didn’t kill anyone.”

“Cat was attacked, as well.”

“I’m well aware of that, and someone could have had darker reasons for the attack than you simply being in the wrong place at the wrong time. I’m not saying you did anything illegal, Cat—at least, I hope you didn’t—but I don’t know that for certain. You and your farm are the common denominators. George Odell ran your barn and Helen Fox vetted your horses. I can't say whether or not you've been involved in whatever it is, but I have to learn the truth of the matter."

"Accusing the lass is ridiculous—"

"It's not an accusation. It's simply something I have to investigate and hopefully rule out."

With a glance out the kitchen window, Cat saw that two police vehicles were coming down her drive and heading for the barn. "What's going on?"

From inside his sports jacket, Pierce pulled out a sheaf of papers. "This is a warrant to search the premises." He put the paperwork on the table and slid it toward her.

"You didn't need a warrant. You can search every inch of the place if it will help you find George's murderer." She glared at it and then glared at him. "I want to nail whoever did it as much as you do. No, *more* than you do. He was family to me."

"And Helen?" Pierce watched her closely.

"I only knew Helen professionally, but of course I want see her killer caught!"

"Good. Evidence techs will be doing a more thorough search on your property this time."

"What will they look for?" Cat asked.

"George's blood, for one."

Cat shuddered and was glad for Aidan's support. She hoped against hope that one of her broodmare owners wouldn't simply show up while the evidence techs were at work. Remembering the argument between Martin and Dean, she knew both men could quickly lose their tempers. That could prove to be a disaster for business.

"So your techs will look for blood in the barn?"

"Everywhere, Cat. Including in this house. I'm sorry, but we have to be thorough. I'll have one of my men stay here with you in the kitchen. You won't be able to go into the other rooms until we're done. Either one of you."

"The lass needs to lie down." Aidan's tone was reasonable. "She was desperately hurt last night."

Pierce gave him an unsympathetic expression. "Then perhaps you'd better take her to a motel."

"I'm not leaving my farm!" Cat said. "If you find something, I want to be here to see it for myself."

Cat stubbornly stayed put despite her throbbing head. She even refused Aidan's idea to get back into the SUV's passenger seat and recline the back so she could rest for a while. The search of her home felt like a personal violation, but she put her own feelings on the back burner. She understood the police had to look at everyone. If only they'd done so when she'd asked. They'd be lucky to find any evidence now.

"What can I get you to eat?" Aidan asked.

"Nothing. My stomach is in too much of a knot to eat. Help yourself, though."

The wait seemed interminable.

Barely an hour later, Pierce himself came back into the house to deliver the news. "We found it. Blood in the barn."

Cat caught her breath. "Mares give birth in that barn."

"It's not anywhere that you'd find that kind of blood. There's a distinct pattern—"

"I want to see it."

"Cat, no!" Aidan protested.

But she was already on her feet and heading toward the back door. She glanced once to make sure Pierce and Aidan were following, then left the house. By the time she got halfway to the barn, her stomach was tied up in knots.

And as she drew closer, she could see the evidence technicians had put up yellow tape around the area they were investigating.

*Crime scene tape.*

"Is that really necessary?" Cat could only imagine the horror her clients would feel when they saw it.

"I'm afraid so," Pierce said. "It shouldn't be there more than a day or so. It's possible we might have to come back to look for additional evidence." When they got to the barn, he lifted the tape and let her and Aidan enter the secured area. "The blood wasn't visible to the naked eye. We used a chemical spray that caused the blood to fluoresce under the right light."

Pierce gave one of the evidence techs the high sign and then shut off the overhead lights. The tech turned on an ultraviolet light and shone it over boards between two aisles. A splatter on the boards glowed in the dark, and to Cat, it looked like a pattern that could have been made when George's head was smashed with a heavy object.

"We found this, as well." Pierce picked up a mucking shovel and held it under the light.

More splatter.

Seeing the murder weapon like this was too much for Cat. Her stomach boiled and she barely made it back outside before heaving the little breakfast she'd eaten at the hospital. Aidan quickly came to her rescue and held her from falling to her knees.

"Sorry about that," the detective said. "You okay?"

Cat glanced at Pierce. "Just great."

"The men are done with your house. Didn't find anything. You can go get some rest now."

"A good idea," Aidan agreed.

But Cat needed to know how things stood. Twin barks alerted her to the imminent arrival of the dogs. "What's next?"

"We have to confirm the blood was your barn

manager's. My men are dusting for fingerprints now."

In their excitement, Smokey and Topaz knocked into her. Bernie wasn't far behind. She said, "You're bound to find all our prints around that area—Raul's, Bernie's, mine. The kids. Even the owners. The same on the shovel handle, since we all use the equipment."

"Maybe we'll find prints that don't belong."

"You found prints?" a wide-eyed Bernie asked.

"And blood. George was struck with a mucking shovel just inside the barn."

"Holy..." Bernie wandered into the entryway to watch the evidence techs at work.

"It's too bad you couldn't find George's suitcase," Cat said. "Maybe the killer's prints would be on it."

"That's right," Pierce said. "When you first called about George being missing, you said he'd packed some of his things and disappeared. What did the case look like?"

Though that had been part of her initial report, she told him again. "A small silvery-gray one with wheels. Like the ones you take on a plane."

"We'll keep an eye out for it," he promised.

Aidan tugged her away from the barn. "Come now, there's nothing more you can do here. You need some rest. And some food."

"I probably ought to make some phone calls."

"Who needs telling?"

"The owners. They're not going to be too happy. They should hear about this from me."

"I am certain Pierce will be talking to them again."

"Great. You should have seen Dean Hill's reaction to the first interview. Now a second murder... both connected to Clarke Acres...he'll go ballistic if Pierce gets to him before I do. I have to call."

"Take a lie-down first. When you are rested, it will go easier."

Too exhausted, too heartsick, to answer, she let him head her for the house. Once inside, she went straight to the bedroom. He didn't follow.

Waiting wouldn't change how the owners reacted to the news of another death, of how Pierce had put it together that she and the farm were somehow at the center of the crime. They could all choose to pick up and move their broodmares to another breeder.

And then where would her business be? In shreds.

Still, she couldn't stand to do it now, so she took Aidan's suggestion. The moment her head hit the pillow, her world floated away.

# *Chapter Sixteen*

Aidan fed Cat leftover pot roast and that afternoon somehow got her through the ordeal of calling her owners. After which, she'd collapsed on the bed again. As much as he wanted to go to the racetrack to check on Mac, Cat might need him.

And later, he slept on the sofa, just in case her attacker returned.

Though he hoped for a dream that would help the investigation, he got nothing this night. Exhausted, he slept like a dead man, waking briefly twice. Both times he looked in on Cat. Watched her sleep. Wondered if he had really condemned her by having sex with a woman who roused his softer emotions.

Convinced that she had somehow been hurt because of him, he vowed never to touch her again.

Would that work?

Could he obliterate the curse from his life and especially from hers somehow?

He didn't know. He only knew that he cared

about her more than he should, and that he was now likely responsible for her very life.

Morning brought with it televised news of the vet's murder. Undoubtedly the story had been picked up on the internet and in the local paper. No mention of Clarke Acres. No cameras set up outside the property or reporters waiting for an interview.

Something for which to be thankful.

At Aidan's prompting, Pierce had agreed to assign a police officer on the farm to guard Cat while Aidan was at the racetrack. The officer showed up as promised at dawn. Having police protection wouldn't last long, Aidan was certain, but at least he could count on it for now.

Even so, he left for the racetrack with a heavy heart and vowed to return as quickly as possible.

The morning workout was Mac's best. He had Nadim take him on several shorter runs to get the colt out of the gate with more power. The race was only ten days away, and still he didn't have a jockey. Cat's attack had put him a day behind schedule. He should at least be talking with potential jockeys or their agents.

Speaking of jockeys…

After the workout, he stood in the shedrow, watching Tim Browne working, not as a jockey but as a hotwalker. The other man circled Mac around the shedrow to cool him off.

What was his game? Aidan wondered.

Why would he leave Ireland for America and hide who he was by taking a commonplace job?

Surely he wasn't involved in whatever was going on at Clarke Acres. Though Aidan wished he could be certain of that.

When the colt was cool enough, Browne brought him back to his stall and turned him loose inside. He told Aidan, "Everyone who has seen Mac run the last few mornings has been impressed."

Smothering his sense of pride for the moment, Aidan couldn't help but bait the man to pry information out of him. "Mac is doing a fine job of it, hopefully good enough to impress a leading jockey into taking the ride."

"'Tis certain he'll attract the attention of someone who will do him justice."

So, still no admission. Had Browne come here to this country, to this very racetrack, in order to secure a ride on Mac? Then why hadn't he just been honest about it?

Browne said, "I haven't seen your partner around the shedrow since the first day."

Aidan started at his interest. "Cat has her own business to run."

"But she has an investment in the colt, as well."

Browne seemed to know more than he should

have, considering he was someone Aidan had met only three days ago.

"Aye, an investment," Aidan agreed, "but broodmares are also in season. She must attend to them first."

"Is that it, then?"

"What else?"

"I heard about the attack. I assume she's recovered."

How did he know about the attack on Cat? Aidan wondered.

Before he could ask, Browne added, "And then there are rumors of murder associated with her farm. I thought perhaps that is why she has stayed away."

"Only inasmuch as the murdered woman vetted her horses as well as those on many other farms."

"Aye, you are correct, of course. Perhaps it was inappropriate of me to speak of it." Browne backed away down the shedrow. "Tell her for me that I sincerely hope she has fully recovered from the attack."

With that Browne escaped.

At least that was the way Aidan saw it.

The edgy conversation with Browne made him wonder if he should warn Cat about his dream, about what had happened to Pegeen.

Would she believe it, though?

She didn't believe in the psychic connection

he had with Mac. She didn't believe in Sheelin O'Keefe's curse. So why would she believe that he had dreams that foretold the future? He couldn't even guarantee things would happen as he'd seen them, when his dreams were filled with half-truths.

And if things didn't happen as he predicted, would she assume he was lying? Like Jack? She'd made it very clear that her ex-husband had been not only a cheater, but a liar, a fact that she'd hated.

If she thought *he* was lying, as well…

If only he could be certain Cat would do as he asked to avoid another tragedy. Or, like Pegeen, would she back up and become more stubborn, would she insist on doing things her way despite anything he had to say?

He didn't want to test it. He wasn't ready to tell Cat about the past, share the awful truth about the way Pegeen had died. He couldn't stand to see Cat turn away from him in disgust.

The best thing, then, would be to hold back his psychic musings and increase his vigilance, so that he could prevent anything bad from happening to another woman about whom he cared.

He would do everything in his power to protect her.

Aidan realized Helen Fox's murder was hot news, but he hadn't seen or read a report link-ing her death to Clarke Acres. And the attack on Cat had been kept from the media, thankfully. So where was Browne getting his information? He supposed it could have come from Raul by way of his brother, Placido. Undoubtedly, Browne knew the other jockey.

Unless…what if Browne himself had been involved in the attack and/or murders?

As unlikely as it seemed, Aidan had to give the idea credence.

BY THE TIME CAT WAS ON HER WAY to the cemetery, she was feeling better. Well-rested, at least. And the throbbing in her head was gone. But her physical well-being had no influence on her feelings.

Her emotions were once more in turmoil, and she had no one to share them with.

She'd dismissed the young policeman who had been dogging her steps all morning—she'd thought he might pass out as he watched her breed Be My Valentine, another of Dean Hill's horses. Aidan was coming to the cemetery straight from the racetrack.

The cemetery was small and well kept, with drifts of flowers in enough areas that it almost looked like a peaceful garden. Most of the plots had markers in the ground or plain headstones. No mausoleums here.

As she drove along the cemetery road, Cat

faced the questions that echoed over and over in her head—who had killed George and why? Did his death really have something to do with her? Or was she simply a chess piece who'd gotten in the way?

No, it all had to be connected: George and Helen both murdered and her knocked out. How were the three separate incidents related?

She thought back to her own attack. Someone had been in the barn late at night, and it wasn't the first time. Though she'd never caught anyone, she'd felt another presence twice before in the past week. Something was going on there without her knowledge.

Something that George must have discovered.

But what about Helen? The vet hadn't been killed in Cat's barn. Was her death really connected?

The unanswered questions plagued her as she pulled up behind several other vehicles near the gravesite. No farm truck. Aidan wasn't here yet.

Raul stood with his hand on the coffin, head bowed as if in prayer, then crossed himself and stepped back to where his brother, Placido, stood. Behind them, she spotted Nadim with a stranger who looked small enough to be another exercise rider or a jockey. Opposite them on the other side of chairs lined up before the coffin, Dean Hill stood with Martin Bradley, his daughter, Simone, and of all people, Jack.

With her stomach clenched and her head going light, hardly able to believe her ex-husband had shown up when he hadn't cared a bit about George, Cat grabbed the photographs she'd taken from her bedroom wall and left the SUV. Where was Aidan? He'd said he would meet her here.

"Miss Clarke, there you are," the funeral director said.

"I have the photographs of George."

Handing them to the man, Cat watched as he set them on the coffin—one photo of the barn manager lunging a horse, the other of him with her whole family at a Fourth of July picnic.

She glanced back to see Bernie arrive. He stopped to say something to Martin, and the man stepped away from his daughter for a moment. It looked as if he and Bernie were arguing about something. Then, tight-lipped, Bernie stalked away and stood by himself while Martin rejoined his group.

What was that about? Cat wondered.

"Is everyone here?" the funeral director asked.

A dark sedan drove up, and Detective Pierce got out. What in the world was he doing here? Surely he didn't intend to conduct a gravesite investigation.

"Not quite everyone," she said, wondering if

Aidan was going to show at all. "Give us a few more minutes."

"Of course."

Pierce stopped at a respectful distance behind the others and turned his gaze from one person to the other. Suspects? Her pulse picked up. Of course he would think that. He'd questioned just about everyone here. And just about everyone here had connections both to George and to Helen.

Cat didn't want to think anyone she knew was guilty of murder, certainly not people she worked with on a daily basis. Not wanting to face the others, especially not her ex-husband, not today, not alone, she turned to the coffin and stared at the photographs and hoped for fond memories of her barn manager to get her through the short service.

The sound of a noisy engine made her turn back to the road to see the farm truck pull up. Not only did Aidan alight, but so did Laura and Vincent. Laura looked scared and Vincent held her hand. The teenagers hung back until a relieved Cat waved them over. Aidan followed. She'd never been so glad to see anyone. A weight lifted from her as he joined her, stopping a yard away and intently studying her face.

"We were just about to start." Giving him as much of a smile as she could muster, she turned to the funeral director and nodded.

"Would everyone gather round?" He motioned everyone closer.

Since there was a single row of chairs, Cat sat in the middle, Aidan on one side of her, the kids on the other. As people took their places, Martin, Simone and Dean sat in the seats on one side, Raul and Bernie on the other. The remaining mourners stood behind the chairs. The hair on the back of Cat's neck stood at attention, making her certain that Jack was directly behind her.

Aidan whispered, "What is Tim Browne doing here?"

Cat glanced back to see Nadim with the stranger. "That's Mac's hotwalker?"

"He's more than a backstretch worker. I will explain later."

Though curious, Cat had to be content with that as the service started. Since George hadn't professed any particular faith and hadn't frequented any church she knew of, Cat had thought it appropriate to let the funeral director conduct the service.

"We are here to bid farewell to George Ordell…"

For a moment, it took all her will for Cat not to cry again. Yes, she was still sad, but more than that, she was angry. Someone had murdered a man who had played a major role in her life. A man about whom she deeply cared. Maybe someone present at this service. That same person had undoubtedly killed Helen Fox, as well. And knocked her out in her own barn.

She looked around, studied the faces, tried to read them. Some wore sorrowful expressions. Some wore no expressions at all. One of the latter was Tim Browne, who stared directly at her, his expression narrowed and probing and making her heart skip a beat.

What was that about?

Strong fingers clasped hers and she looked down to see Aidan holding her hand as if to give her strength. She clung to that and thought only of George through the end of the short service.

And as the coffin was lowered into the ground, Cat swore she would help bring the killer to justice.

THROUGHOUT THE SERVICE, Aidan had the distinct feeling that not everyone was here out of fondness for George Odell. Or even for Cat, for that matter.

Strong, dark vibes assaulted him, but he didn't know from which direction. From Cat's ex, perhaps?

From the murderer?

He could not help but notice the way Tim Browne had been studying Cat. And he could not help but be irritated by the presence of the man who had no reason to be here. The man was not showing his support because he was working with Mac, of that he was certain.

And so when the service was over, and goodbyes were being said, he whispered in Cat's ear, "Can you take Laura and Vincent back to the farm?"

"Of course."

"Then I'll meet you there in a while. I have something I need to take care of first."

Cat nodded, and he squeezed her arm and then rushed to catch up to Browne before the man could get in Nadim's car.

"Wait. We need to talk."

"Tomorrow at the track."

"Now. Here."

Browne looked at Nadim. "Can you give us a few minutes?"

"Certainly." Nadim took his cell phone from his pocket and turned it on. "I need to check my messages anyway."

"This way."

Aidan moved away from the vehicles and people on the cemetery road. He stopped in the shelter of a shade tree, several inches of mulch beneath his feet.

"What can I be doing for you, Mr. McKenna?"

"Tell me why you're here."

"Out of respect, of course."

"You knew the deceased?"

"No. Never met the man. But I know you and through you, Miss Clarke."

"How exactly do you know me? What is it you want of me?"

"I don't understand."

The time for pretence was over. Aidan was going to get to the heart of the matter. "I am not one for coincidence. We both come from Ireland and we both end up at the same racetrack in the middle of America at virtually the same time. Explain that to me."

"I fear I cannot."

"Cannot or will not?" When Browne went silent, Aidan said, "Then explain why a jockey is working as a hotwalker."

Browne's expression tightened. "You know who I am, then."

"I know you were racing in Southern Australia for the last several years, that you came back to Ireland and left again to come here. But not as a jockey. That takes some explaining." When the jockey didn't try, Aidan nearly exploded with frustration. "You came because of me, did you not? What was the plan? To ruin my partnership with Cat? Or to make me look like a murderer?"

"You're daft, man!"

"Am I? Then explain yourself."

At first, Aidan didn't think he would. Browne seemed torn, ready to leave as were the other mourners. Several vehicles passed them on the way to the exit.

And then Browne said, "I came because of Pegeen."

Which took away Aidan's breath. That was the last thing he'd expected to hear.

"You knew Pegeen?" Not a stretch, since Pegeen had been a jockey like Browne.

"She was my sister."

Aidan started. "Pegeen had two sisters, no brother. And her last name was Flynn, not Browne."

"She was my half sister. Several years after Da died, my mother remarried. She and her new husband had three daughters. Pegeen was the youngest, so there was more than a decade between us. The only thing we shared was our love of horses. I taught her what I could about being a jockey, but I was already in Australia when she got her first ride."

"I can check on your story."

"You do that, then."

Aidan studied the man's face. He'd thought Tim Browne looked familiar and now he knew why. He saw traces of the woman he'd once loved in the determined jaw and the set of his mouth.

"So you followed me here why?"

"You were leaving Ireland just as I was about to meet you there."

"You came back from Australia to meet me?"

"To see what kind of a man you were. Whether or not you were responsible for my sister's death."

"What took you so long, then? Why did you not come home for your sister's funeral?"

"I was in no shape to travel. I was recuperating from surgeries to repair my leg and remove my spleen. The more I thought on Pegeen's death, however, the more I had to find out for myself whether or not you were responsible."

"I was," Aidan admitted, because it was true. Guilt flooded him. "I loved your sister, and 'tis my fault she died."

Browne stared in silence for a moment, then said, "I wanted to know what kind of trainer you were. Whether you would push a jockey to do something careless. I did not accuse you of anything more."

"'Tis the truth of the matter. I didn't stop her from riding PushedToTheLimit."

"So you knew there was something wrong with the colt?"

"There was nothing wrong with him. 'Twas a bad ride and they got caught between two horses, is what happened."

"Then how was that your fault? How is it you think you killed her?"

"Because I saw it happen and didn't stop it."

"Saw it?"

"In a dream." Aidan waited for a reaction, and when he got none, continued, "Not her dying, but the accident itself. The morning she died, I told

Pegeen about it and asked her to beg off the ride. She simply laughed. She didn't believe in such warnings."

And undoubtedly neither would her brother, though he noticed Browne didn't seem in the least amused.

"You have the sight, then."

Browne gave it credence, Aidan thought. "Of a sort." He still couldn't bring himself to talk about the curse. "I can't always trust the dreams that come to me. That's why I hesitated doing what I should have in order to stop the disaster from happening."

"Pegeen did what she wanted. A more stubborn lass never existed. If she wanted to ride, nothing would have stopped her."

"I could have pulled the colt. At the last minute, I could have said there was something medically wrong with PushedToTheLimit and pulled him from the schedule."

"But when the vet checked him out afterward, he wouldn't find anything wrong. Making the wrong call might have ruined you."

"Do you think that's what mattered to me?" Aidan hadn't even thought of the repercussion to himself. "I cared about your sister. I cared about ending the colt's career before it even started. I cared about letting down the owner who trusted me. There were too many things to consider. I could have been wrong. I knew that. I took too long to decide."

Browne stared at him intently, as if he were trying to get inside Aidan's soul. Though Pegeen's brother made him uncomfortable, Aidan allowed it. And if Browne wanted revenge for his sister, Aidan wouldn't stop him.

The man finally said, "It sounds to me like you did nothing wrong."

"You're not the one who has to live with the uncertainty." And the never-ending guilt.

"I came here to see that Pegeen got justice…if I found it was warranted," Browne admitted. "As I see it, you did nothing wrong, and yet you punish yourself more than anyone else ever could."

Sensing they weren't alone, Aidan looked past Browne to see Nadim standing a few yards away. He was wearing an impatient expression.

"Nadim wants to leave."

Browne glanced back. "I'll be right there." To Aidan he said, "Perhaps you should find another hotwalker."

"I am so deeply sorry about Pegeen."

Browne nodded. "My sister would not want you to make your life about what happened to her. She would want you to get on with it and be happy." With that, he left.

Leaving Aidan wondering if Pegeen had sent her brother to ease his conscience and free him to do exactly that.

## *Chapter Seventeen*

Cat had brought the kids back to the farm and had spent more than an hour doing manual labor alongside them. After which, she'd let them take the horses out to make up for the wretched day.

Now showered, her hair washed, she stood in the living room, staring out the window toward the barn.

"How are you, really?" Aidan asked.

"As well as can be expected, I guess, considering the authorities don't seem to be getting anywhere with this case."

"Investigations take time."

Behind her, he placed his hands on her shoulders, making her want to melt back against him. She said, "It's been time enough for a second murder."

"Pierce has only been at it a few days."

He should have been at it a few weeks, but there was no use in bringing that up again. "And it's clear that I'm somehow involved."

"Not you. Your farm."

"I'm the one who was knocked out."

"Because you foolishly went to the barn alone in the middle of the night and interrupted something criminal."

"That won't happen again," she promised. "And whatever is going on there, I've got it covered."

"Meaning?"

"I reset the video cameras, the ones meant to help me keep an eye from the house on the mares ready to give birth. The foaling stalls on the other side of the main aisles are double-size so the mares have enough room. And each stall is rigged with two cameras. I adjusted them to look over the whole barn. I can check on the barn all night from the office next to my bedroom."

The clop-clop of horses' hooves and excited voices made Cat turn back to the window.

"Laura and Vincent are back from their ride already." And they were coming toward the house rather than the barn. "That's odd. They usually stay out as long as possible."

"What is that Vincent is carrying?" Aidan asked.

Cat focused on the bulky object he balanced in front of him on the saddle. "Oh, my…I think that's George's suitcase!"

"SO YOU FETCHED THIS from the stream?" Pierce asked.

Cat had called the detective the moment the excited teenagers had brought the suitcase to her. She'd been through this with them while waiting for Pierce to arrive. Now it was his turn to repeat the questions she and Aidan had already asked. They and the kids sat at the kitchen table, while Pierce did a cursory inspection of the rolling case that sat on the floor halfway between them and the back door. She had to keep the dogs in check. As with anything that smelled odd, they kept wanting to investigate for themselves.

"It was stuck on a tree limb," Vincent said, "like the storm had thrown it there."

"Where exactly did you find it?"

Vincent and Laura looked at each other, and Cat saw something secretive pass between them.

Reaching across the table to give Laura's hand a squeeze, Vincent continued to do the talking. "Downstream from the ravine."

"And you just rode by and saw it?"

"Well, not exactly."

The kids exchanged another look.

Laura made a face and admitted, "We were, uh, swimming."

Pierce gave them a once-over. "But your clothes are dry."

"Yeah, well, we weren't exactly wearing them," Vincent said.

"We weren't naked!" Laura was quick to add.

Cat noted the teenager's face flushed with embarrassment, but she said nothing.

"So, do you think you will get fingerprints from the case?" Aidan asked.

"The outside? Doubtful. It's been through a lot of weather, a lot of water." The detective turned to Cat. "You can identify this case for certain as belonging to George Odell, though, right?"

"If I'm wrong, all you have to do is open it to find out."

"At the lab. You never know what we might find inside." He picked up the filthy wet case with gloved hands and headed for the door. "You'll be hearing from me."

"I'm sure I will." She waited until the detective left before giving the kids her fiercest expression. "Skinny-dipping?" Not that she was a prude, but while they were here, whether working for her or otherwise, she was the responsible adult. "What do you think your parents will say about that?"

Laura squealed. "You can't tell them!"

"I wasn't planning on it…as long as you tell me you won't do that again, not while you're taking my horses out."

"We won't!" both teenagers promised.

Aidan said, "That does not speak to Detective Pierce's discretion, however."

"Oh, great, Vincent." Laura sounded as if she were ready to cry. "I told you we were going to get in trouble."

"Yeah, well, it didn't take long to convince you to take that chance."

Her face deepening to a beet-red, Laura smacked Vincent in the arm, and when she ran out of the kitchen, he was directly behind her.

"C'mon, I was just teasing you!" he yelled as he went out the back door.

Apparently thinking they were playing, the dogs squeezed out the door before it slammed.

"Young love," Aidan said.

"Love has no age limit, and I fear it never gets easier."

Or so it seemed to her. Though she'd tried to put Jack out of mind, he kept inserting himself back into her life, reminding her of how gullible she had been, how willing to accept what he'd said on faith.

And now her growing feelings for Aidan scared her silly.

What if she was wrong about him, too?

She was giving herself a hard time for nothing—it was far too soon to decide where their relationship was or was not headed.

"I wonder how long it will take Pierce to have his people check out the suitcase."

"Even if he learns something, he may not tell us until he has enough to arrest the murderer."

"If it even gives him enough to go on. Fingerprints. Hair. Whatever. If the person responsible has never been arrested, he'll never make a match."

"'Tis the only thing we have to go on."

"For now. I'll just have to be patient." She sighed. "And keep busy."

"Do you not think you have done enough for the day? Perhaps you need to take it easy."

"And go crazy thinking about it? I need to check on the mares anyway. I no longer have a vet, so until I have time to get a new one, it's up to me to decide when a mare is pregnant and whether or not it's time to breed one."

Cat didn't want to think about having to repeat today's experience. At least Helen's family was planning the wake and funeral, but Cat would of course attend both. Helen had been not only her vet, but a friend.

"What can I do to help?" Aidan asked.

"With the mares? Nothing. But you could do something about dinner."

"You want me to cook? 'Tis a request you may regret."

"Actually, I was thinking of takeout. There's a

place in town just off the square called the Italian Villa. It has great pasta and even better pizza. If you like Italian."

"Sounds grand."

She told him how to find it. "Take your time. I should be done in an hour or so, but sometimes checking on the horses takes longer than I expect."

"I'm familiar with that particular problem."

Cat was glad to see him go. She needed some time alone to process. It had been quite a day. She'd bred a horse. She'd buried an old friend. She'd possibly identified the link to the murderer.

If only she could do more to nail whoever had killed George and Helen. It had to be the same person. The same person who'd been doing something secretive in her barn and had knocked her out. Someone who'd come to the gravesite to look innocent?

Moments flitted through her mind. The cast of mourners, for example. Aidan had never told her what he'd had to say to Tim Browne, or what it was he'd wanted to tell her when he'd arrived. *More than a backstretch worker*—what did that mean? He'd never explained. Afterward, he'd merely said Browne had come to pay his respects.

Placido being there had confused her, as well. He might have met George when he'd come to see his brother, but he hadn't really known the barn manager. Undoubtedly, he'd simply wanted to impress Mac's owner. Or at least to become more visible to Aidan.

What was Jack's reason for showing up to the burial of someone he didn't even like? Quite possibly he'd simply wanted to torture her. Or to somehow impress his future father-in-law. Unless, of course, *he* was the murderer, there to see what people suspected, something she really didn't want to believe.

And then there was Martin's argument with Bernie. Had Bernie done something with Martin's horses that the owner hadn't liked? Bernie had denied being in the barn late at night when she'd asked, but he'd raised her suspicions. And Jack had used him to establish how long he'd been in the barn while she was in Ireland.

She might call Martin to feel him out about the argument, but she couldn't forget that he was a suspect, as was every other person at the burial.

Other than the kids, of course.

The thought stuck with her. Bernie was always friendly with both Vincent and Laura—perhaps because he was the youngest full-time employee and had gone to high school with their older siblings.

So when she was done in the barn and went back to the house, and Aidan and dinner were nowhere in sight, she decided to call Vincent.

"Hey, Miss Clarke, sorry about before—"

"That's not why I'm calling." Despite her worries, Cat kept her tone as even as she could manage. "I wanted to ask you about Bernie."

"Why? What did he do?"

"I don't know. That's what I'm trying to find out. At the cemetery today, he and Mr. Bradley were having words. I'm worried Bernie did something to make Mr. Bradley angry."

"That wouldn't be too hard."

"Bernie doing something he shouldn't have? Or Mr. Bradley getting angry easily?"

"Both, them being related and all."

A statement that shocked Cat into silence for a moment. Then she asked, "Related? How?"

"You didn't know Mr. Bradley is Bernie's uncle?"

News to her. "No."

"Mr. Bradley is the one who told Bernie about the job. But he makes Bernie miserable anytime he's around. I guess he's pretty critical."

"You've heard them argue before?"

"Only once. But Bernie said his uncle was on his back a lot lately, making him do stuff he didn't want to do."

"Like what?" It was getting harder to sound normal. "Things around here?"

"He didn't say."

"Thanks, Vincent. Do me a favor and don't say anything to Bernie about this. I wouldn't want to embarrass him."

"Well, yeah, I guess I owe you one," he said, lowering his voice. "Since you're not going to say anything to Laura's and my parents and all."

"And I won't, since you're going to keep your promise not to skinny-dip again and all." Hearing the truck coming up the drive, she used it as her excuse to end the conversation. "Ah, dinner has arrived. I'll see you tomorrow, Vincent."

When Aidan entered the kitchen, his arms and hands were full. "I hope you're hungry."

Hoping they were in for a treat, the dogs crowded them.

"Good grief, you bought out the restaurant. You must be starving."

"That I am. Truthfully, I could not decide what to get, so I just bought everything that appealed. And I know how to use a micro to warm up left-over food."

Cat smiled for the first time that day. "A good talent to have."

When they set out the food on the table—stuffed-sausage pizza, calamari, fettuccini alfredo with shrimp, gnocchi in marinara sauce, Caesar salad and garlic bread—there was hardly room enough for them. Smokey and Topaz sat between them, hopeful gazes going from one human to the other.

As they ate, Cat allowed herself to enjoy the food and Aidan's company. She was getting used to having him around. Having him in her bed. Not the night before, though. He'd said she needed to sleep without him disturbing her, but was that really it? Something had been bothering him, was bothering him now. She saw past the banter and the smile.

His eyes told of a different mood.

A mood that carried through the evening as he helped her clear the table and then escorted her to the barn for a good-night check on the mares.

A mood that followed him back into the house where he announced his intention to sleep on her sofa again.

Feeling vulnerable, Cat wished him into her bed. But still, he never appeared. Alone with only the dogs to keep her company, she stared up into the dark, wondering what had changed between them.

Had her growing feelings for Aidan scared him away?

She was scared, and not only of a murderer being on the loose. Had she been wrong about Aidan's feelings for her in the first place?

She couldn't stand the thought of being broken by love again.

*HER MIND WAS GOING IN circles as she checked on all the horses. She kept trying to focus, but her thoughts kept wandering back to the cemetery. To finding George. To imagining what horror Helen must have felt when she'd been euthanized like an animal.*

*She shuddered. Would the nightmare never end? Dread filled her but she continued working, hurrying to finish. Hurrying to put distance between her and whatever was frightening her.*

*Then she tried hurrying from the barn, from the invisible threat that frightened her, but a sharp pain in her back stopped her cold. Her legs gave out and she fell facedown on the stable floor. She lay there, unable to move, her thoughts hazy. A commotion from nearby told her one of the horses was in danger.*

*Hooves crashed against stall boards, followed by an almost human scream...*

The scream carried into real time…one of the horses…

Aidan nearly fell off the couch in his hurry to check on Cat. He didn't take a breath until he saw her there, safe in her bed. Though she was sleeping, she must have been dreaming, as well, for she thrashed…settled…thrashed some more.

What nightmares plagued *her* sleep?

He wanted in the worst way to slip into bed

with her and take her in his arms…to comfort her…to love her.

Instead, he shook away his own longing and entered the office farther down the hall to check the monitors hooked up to the cameras in the barn. The barn was dark as it had been last time he'd checked, so there was nothing to see. That horse's scream had been all in his head. Nothing going on there. He could barely make out the movement of a few restless horses.

Disappointed for multiple reasons, he returned to the couch. This wasn't about what *he* wanted; it was about keeping Cat safe from Sheelin's damn curse.

If only he could get her to believe.

Then he could warn her, tell her about the dream that was so like the first one he'd had. Similar but different. Some things had changed—time of day, sensory details—but in the end she was drugged, as she had been in the first dream. Could he still be mixing up the danger to Cat with what had happened to the vet?

He shook his head. It was all too fuzzy, too unspecific. Cat would never believe him. Even if she did, what did he expect her to do? Walk away from her business? Go somewhere to hide until the killer was caught?

If she would do it, he would go with her.

And then a plan took shape in his mind.

If Cashel weren't so far off in Ireland, Aidan would call his older brother and tell him what he decided he had to do to protect Cat.

For a moment, he considered his options.

Tiernan was far away, as well, but South Dakota wasn't "Ireland" far. He could catch a flight and be here by end of day tomorrow. The youngest McKenna brother had worked with the business until two years ago, and he'd helped train Mac when the colt had been a yearling. Tiernan could represent McKenna Racing and take over for him as Mac's trainer for the upcoming stakes race.

Tiernan had fought the curse and won. He and Ella were happily married. Once Aidan told him what was happening, Tiernan would surely agree to do whatever he could to help.

Aidan checked the time. Hours before dawn. Earlier in South Dakota. Too early to call and wake his brother. He would wait for a decent hour. Tiernan would need his sleep to have his wits about him.

In the meantime, Aidan would get things in order. Leaving a police officer to guard Cat again during the day, he would go to the racetrack for the morning training session, after which he would make the call. And then at last he would hire a jockey. Once Tiernan arrived, Aidan would kidnap Cat if necessary, and take her somewhere the murderer could never find her.

She might hate him for it, but at least she would be alive.

## *Chapter Eighteen*

By the time Cat awoke, sometime before noon, Aidan had left for the track. In his place on the couch was a different police officer than the one who'd shadowed her the day before. Stretched out, glued to a televised news show, he barely seemed to notice she was up and about. One glance at her and his gaze returned to his program.

Going about her business, Cat caught a quick lunch, fed the dogs, then headed out for the barn.

"I'm getting to work now," she called back to him.

Had he even noticed she'd left?

The dogs went off on their daily rounds and she entered the barn. Not having some stranger trailing her around, asking questions and getting queasy watching her work as had happened the morning before was a relief. She could get more work done if she didn't have to explain herself every few minutes.

As she began with Dean's mares, she found it

hard to tell whether or not Fairy Tail had conceived. If not, Dean would be disappointed that his streak had ended. Diamond Dame was looking good, but it was too soon for Cat to tell if the mare had taken. Be My Valentine, the mare she'd bred the day before, seemed a little skittish this morning. Reminded of the way Fairy Tail had acted the night after being bred, Cat checked Valentine over thoroughly but found no reason to be concerned.

Her restless night had her jumping out of bed nearly every hour to check the monitors in her office, only to see nothing. The barn had remained dark. Apparently nothing untoward had gone on here last night. Nothing to worry her.

Thinking that she—and the horses—were all safe, Cat nearly jumped out of her skin when she left Valentine's stall only to run into Bernie, who held a mucking shovel in hand.

Heart thumping, she asked, "Why didn't you say something? You could scare someone to death."

"Sorry. I was just trying to do my job." As if to prove it, he entered the stall on the opposite side of the aisle.

He sounded out of sorts. Remembering her conversation with Vincent, Cat asked, "Something troubling you?"

Bernie merely grunted in return and heaved a

shovelful of manure into the wheelbarrow he'd left in the aisle.

"I understand your uncle has been riding you."

"My uncle?"

"Martin Bradley is your uncle, right?"

That stopped him dead. "Uh, yeah. How did you find out?"

"I didn't know it was supposed to be a secret."

"Well, it's not. I just thought you might not hire me if you knew I was related to your best client."

"Why wouldn't I?"

"I don't know."

Realizing he sounded irritated, Cat tried again. "So was the argument at the cemetery something serious?"

Bernie stared at her, openmouthed, his eyes widening slightly. "No, of course not. Uncle Martin just likes to run things his way."

Did he mean personally or here at the farm? Cat chose not to ask.

"Just remember that I'm your employer, and I haven't had any complaints about your work. I think you do a great job around here."

Flushing, Bernie looked away from her, mumbling, "Thanks."

Was he embarrassed by the compliment or because he was doing something he shouldn't… something his uncle had asked him to do?

"Sometimes you just need someone to talk to, Bernie. I'm a pretty good listener."

His grunting in response and hefting another shovelful of manure to the wheelbarrow ended the conversation in Cat's mind. It opened another flood of questions—like whether or not she ought to be working in the barn with Bernie and no other witnesses. Maybe she should go back to the house and remind the cop of why he was there.

But as she approached the open doors, she saw him sitting beneath a tree between house and barn. So he was on the job, after all, if not willing to spend his time in the barn looking over her shoulder. That suited her just fine.

She switched aisles and checked on Martin's horses next. Another few days and she should know whether or not Sweetpea Sue was pregnant. She hoped so. Martin seemed to be losing faith in her because his other mares hadn't conceived with the first cover. He seemed a little desperate. What was that about, and what was he asking Bernie to do that had caused an argument at the cemetery? Bernie had been anything but forthcoming, which made her decidedly uneasy.

About to take care of her own horses—they could all use some time out in the pasture, and so she headed for the back aisle to open the gate—Cat realized Raul had entered the barn and was preparing buckets of feed. Looking decidedly unhappy, he left what he was doing to talk to her.

"Miss Clarke, Placido called me, said you're not giving him the ride in the stakes race."

Certain that Aidan had good reason to eliminate Raul's brother—after finding the matches from Fernando's Hideaway and then seeing the jockey there and learning their other brother owned the place, Cat didn't trust him much herself—she said, "The decision wasn't up to me."

"Mr. McKenna hired someone named Tim Browne to ride Mac Finnian."

Unable to hide her surprise, she started. "The hotwalker?"

"That's what my brother said. What kind of craziness is this? It's not right, Miss Clarke. Even if this guy got his jockey's license, what does anyone know about him? Placido earned his ranking at the track. He deserves the chance. Not some wannabe jockey hotwalker. Can't you talk to Mr. McKenna, get him to change his mind?"

"Indeed I will speak with Aidan about it." Not that she would recommend Placido. "You know he has the final say as to who rides Mac Finnian. He is the trainer."

"But you're the backer," Raul argued. "He wouldn't be here without you."

At the cemetery, Aidan had said Tim Browne was more than a backstretch worker, but he'd never explained that he was a jockey. In the meantime, she didn't want bad feelings with Raul, so she tried to smooth things over.

"I'll let you know if Aidan will reconsider."

Scowling, Raul nodded and went back to his feed. Cat realized Bernie was just bringing his empty wheelbarrow back inside and probably had overheard their exchange.

She opened the pasture gate, then made for the center aisle and her horses. Just before she reached the first stall, something underfoot crunched. She looked down to see what she'd stepped on. It looked like broken glass. Stooping, she carefully picked up several of the pieces—thin and straw-like. Her heart began to pound.

Just then, she realized Bernie was standing a short way off and staring.

"Broken glass," she said, forcing herself to stay calm. "Do you know anything about this?"

"Me? No!"

Her employees knew better than to bring glass into the barn.

Especially this type of glass.

Not knowing what else to do, she scooped it up with gloved hands and threw it in the trash. Though she scoured the barn floor, she didn't find more glass.

Looking back, she realized Bernie had disappeared.

Cat stood there a moment, trying to decide what to do.

How could she go on, acting like this was just another day? That's what she'd been trying to do since learning George had been murdered. She'd been putting one foot in front of the other, continuing on with her business and her life as if nothing had happened.

As if Helen hadn't been put down like an animal.

As if she herself hadn't been knocked out.

And now this.

How could she trust anyone associated with her own barn?

Realizing what she'd just done, she bent over the trash and got a hand on some of that broken glass, scooped it back up and carried it with her to the house where she found a plastic bag, dropped in the shards, put the small bundle into her shoulder bag, threw the gloves on the sink and left.

"Where are you headed?" the cop asked as she made for her vehicle.

He was on his feet, apparently ready to go with her.

"Racetrack," she said.

"Hey, I'm willing. I got a couple of extra twenties in my wallet."

Upset by his casual tone and the big grin, she

got into the SUV. "If you want to bet on some races, take your own car!"

Cat needed to find Aidan to tell him about what she'd found. She roared off the property and focused on getting to the track's backstretch as fast as she could. She made it in eleven minutes flat.

After parking in back of the shedrow, Cat ran for Mac's stall. No colt. No Aidan. Being that the track was in the midst of its late-afternoon races, they might be at the practice track. To be certain, she decided to call to find out. She'd barely pulled the phone from her pocket when she heard the Irish lilt.

"C'mon, boyo, you and me are going to become best friends."

She turned to see Tim Browne leading the black colt back to his stall. "Excuse me, but where can I find Aidan?"

"He left for the airport ten minutes ago."

"Airport?"

"Aye. His brother is flying in and Aidan went to fetch him."

Cashel was in from Ireland? What was going on? Why hadn't Aidan told her? Feeling her adrenaline deflate, Cat turned to go back to her vehicle. What did she do now?

"Miss Clarke, if you can spare a moment..."

Though impatient, Cat waited to see what he

wanted. He put Mac into his stall and gave the colt a peppermint, then turned his attention to her.

"I promise you, I will put my all into making Mac Finnian into the champion he deserves to be."

"I certainly hope so." She couldn't keep a tiny note of uncertainty from her tone. "I thought you were a hotwalker."

"No need to fret, I have my jockey's license. Everything is legal. I have been a jockey for more than a decade. I took the hotwalker job simply to be at this track when McKenna brought the colt in from Galway."

"You took that kind of a chance so you could convince Aidan to let you ride Mac Finnian?"

"'Twasn't my idea at all. Truthfully, I was surprised when he asked me to do it this morning. I came to America simply to see what kind of trainer Aidan McKenna really was."

"I don't understand."

"If he hasn't said anything yet, I suppose he will, so no harm in telling you that Pegeen Flynn was my half sister. I was laid up in Australia when her horse broke down under her. I had to be certain her death was not on McKenna's head."

Cat's breath caught in her throat. "Pegeen...she was a jockey?"

He nodded. "My influence, I fear. And when she met McKenna, she lost all sense of care for her own safety. She was so determined to win for him."

It dawned on Cat. "They had a personal relationship."

"Indeed, they were in love. McKenna still carries guilt on his shoulders for her death."

Her stomach knotted at his words and she could only listen in shock.

"I have seen him at work these last days," Browne went on. "One of the best trainers I've ever known. He would never take a chance with someone's life. 'Twas my sister's own stubbornness on having the ride despite McKenna's warning that killed her."

"There was something wrong with the horse?"

He shook his head. "Considering the short time you have worked together, I guess you would not know everything about your business partner. Aidan McKenna has the sight. He saw the accident to come and did his best to talk Pegeen off the horse. My sister was the down-to-earth one in the family. No sense of whimsy or of anything she couldn't see or touch. She never even believed talk of fairy creatures when she was a wee lass. McKenna warned her, but she did not believe him."

As he spoke, Cat went cold inside. Aidan loved another woman. A dead woman. He hadn't told her about Pegeen. He hadn't told her about Tim Browne, either. He hadn't told her that his brother was flying in. He certainly hadn't told her about having the sight.

Would she have believed him? She might have allowed his claim to having a psychic connection with Mac, but she'd scoffed at the idea of a love curse.

She remembered the end of that conversation with him:

*"But no one died."*

*"Not that time, because Da avoided the curse."*

*What other time was he referring to?*

She still wondered about that "other time." Did Aidan think he'd brought this curse down on Pegeen?

What else hadn't Aidan told her?

Shaken to her core, Cat backed away. "I'm sorry for your loss," she whispered, and then fled the scene.

Somehow, she got herself back to the farm in one piece. Aidan wasn't there, of course. He was at the airport. When had he been planning to tell her about Cashel flying in from Ireland?

Had he ever planned on telling her the woman he loved had died for him?

AIDAN DROVE HIS BROTHER Tiernan and sister-in-law Ella first to the track, where he gave them a quick tour and got Tiernan to sign his paperwork so that he could be recognized as a trainer for McKenna

Racing. Before leaving, he introduced his brother to Nadim and Tim Browne.

After which he drove to a car rental company and then led the way to a chain motel on the main road between the track and town.

Once inside the room, Aidan clasped his brother to him. "Thank you for coming to the rescue, Tiernan. And you, Ella."

The photographs Tiernan had emailed him didn't do Ella justice. Half Lakota, she had the best of both worlds in her beautiful face.

"Of course we would do anything to help you," she said. "After all, Tiernan and I beat the odds to be together. We want to see you happy, as well."

"After losing Pegeen, I never thought I would be happy again. But being with Cat has given me a new hope for the future. Now I fear losing her, as well."

"Then why haven't you told her?" Tiernan asked.

Thinking about how wound up her ex-husband could make Cat, he said, "I don't think she's ready for love."

"You wouldn't be honest even for her own protection?" Ella asked.

"I told her about Sheelin's curse. She didn't believe me."

"But you did not tell her about your dreams, boyo."

"She would not believe that, either, Tiernan. Not that it matters. I will not let her fall to the curse. I must protect her, even if it means stealing her away until the murderer is caught."

He noted the look of understanding that passed between his brother and sister-in-law.

Tiernan said, "Promise you will keep us informed of your whereabouts."

"Aye. And I will inform you if she agrees to let you oversee the farm while we are gone."

Though hopefully it would be only a few days, someone had to be in charge, and as far as he was concerned, both Raul and Bernie were suspect. There was no one to be trusted other than his own brother.

His only regret that it wasn't likely he would see Mac run the stakes race, Aidan left to carry out the second part of his plan. He hoped that Cat would understand, not fight him, but that didn't seem likely, either.

Then his hope was that she wouldn't hate him for what he was about to do.

STILL STUNNED when she arrived back at the farm, Cat stumbled out of the SUV and looked around. No farm truck. No car belonging to Vincent. No police car.

The place looked deserted.

The sound of a horse screaming split the silence. No thought to her own safety, she ran to the barn. The horses were her life. Her responsibility. She wouldn't let anyone hurt them.

Once inside, she stopped. Snapped on the overhead lights. Looked around for anything out of place. Listened intently for another indication of trouble. Some of the horses were on edge, moving around their stalls, making low sounds of discontent.

One kicked the stall boards.

Another snorted.

A third squealed.

Her senses came alive as she walked down the main aisle, checking her own horses first. Why were they all so upset?

And then she heard another scream—it came from her stallion.

Dangerous Illusion was more than a little anxious. He kicked the stall boards. Squealed. Kicked again. A rumble set through the barn, the other horses responding to his unease.

She stopped outside his stall. "What's wrong, boy? What has you going?"

His eyes rolled and he threw back his head and banged his hip into the stall wall hard enough to make it shake.

And Cat knew he'd been drugged. She guessed with some kind of opiate that was making him nervous and aggressive.

"What the hell?"

What could she do to bring him down? She didn't even have a vet now. If he kept up like this, he could break a leg. Or worse. What if his heart gave out?

She had to get help.

Hurrying down the aisle, sensing an invisible threat, she tripped over her own feet when something sharp plunged into her back. She tried to turn, to see the face of her attacker. But before she could do so, her legs gave out and she fell face-down on the barn floor.

Unable to move…

Wondering if she, too, was about to be euthanized.

## *Chapter Nineteen*

Aidan parked the truck at the barn. Getting out, he called, “Cat, are you in there?”

His only response was a snort and squeal from one of the horses.

“Cat?” He stood in the open doorway. “Raul? Bernie?”

No answer. Where was everyone? Cat’s SUV was parked near the house. Perhaps she’d decided to get some rest. Or some food. He crossed to the back door.

The kitchen was empty. Not even the dogs to great him.

“Cat?” he called, then went straight to her bedroom, but she wasn’t there, either.

Now he was trying not to worry. Undoubtedly she was out on the property with the dogs. And maybe with her workers. They could be doing fencing repairs or bringing bales of hay in from storage, for all he knew.

About to take out the truck to search for her,

he hesitated, then decided to check her office and the video feeds from the barn before leaving. The barn lights were off, but there was enough daylight for the cameras to pick up images. Wide shots on the two monitors together allowed him to see the whole interior of the stable area.

For some reason, the horses were restless, unusually so.

He searched for the cause, quickly finding the heart of the disturbance that led him straight to Cat's stallion. He was moving around his stall, lunging, throwing his head, kicking the boards. Totally agitated, but why?

Then he saw it, the bit of yellow on the stall floor.

The camera angle didn't allow a clear view, but that didn't stop his pulse from plunging straight into his throat. An arm—that was an arm wearing a yellow pullover like the one he'd seen before, he was certain of it.

*Cat's arm...*

Aidan ran from the house and made straight for the barn, praying he wasn't too late, that the stallion hadn't stomped her and hurt her or worse. Cat had to be hurt, or why would she be down? What had the horse done to her?

Bursting through the open barn doors, he ran down the center aisle, his gut in knots, his heart pounding.

"Cat!" he yelled as he ran. "Say something to me!"

*Be alive, please!*

Reaching the stallion's stall, Aidan realized Dangerous Illusion had worked himself into a state. The stallion was unnaturally agitated, making Aidan think he was on a drug-induced high. There was no opening the door with him like that, not with Cat lying there directly in his path. The stallion would no doubt charge him to get away, and in the process run over her.

Aidan wished he'd brought Tiernan with him—his brother's connection with horses was far stronger than his own. There was no helping it. He concentrated on the stallion—his heart rate was too fast, his vision distorted, the inside of his mind frenzied. Hoping he wasn't too far gone to be reached, Aidan projected calming images of rolling pastures accompanied by soft words.

*'Tis all right, lad. Slow down now. Take a breath. Smell the fresh hay. See the beauty of the pasture surrounding you.*

His psychic connection might not be as strong as his brother's, but Aidan could feel the stallion responding to his hypnotic internal voice.

*That's it. Let your mind rest. Take it easy now, lad.*

He couldn't wait any longer to get Cat out of the stall, so he carefully opened the gate.

*I'm coming in. Stay where you are. That's the lad. No one is going to hurt you.*

Aidan slipped inside the stall and dropped down next to Cat. He felt for a pulse. She was alive and apparently uninjured. He'd gotten to her in time, before she'd been trampled. Carefully, he scooped her up into his arms. She murmured something and tried to open her eyes.

"'Tis all right, Cat. I have you." He eased back from the stallion, whose flesh quivered.

*That's the lad. Relax. Let your mind settle and slow.*

Cat's eyes blinked open and, appearing to be shocked, she tried pushing him away. "Don't."

"Cat, 'tis Aidan," he said softly, so as not to agitate the stallion. "You are safe now."

She stopped pushing, but her expression remained wary, as if she had some reason to distrust him.

"What happened?" she asked.

Once in the aisle, he managed to close the stall gate. "You can't remember?"

She blinked again and her forehead pulled. "Pain. Sharp. In my back. Then everything went dark."

As had happened in his dream. He was doing the right thing, then.

"Can you stand?"

"I think so."

Setting her on her feet, he held on to her.

"O-oh, I'm a little dizzy."

"Someone drugged you."

"And my stallion. He was so agitated, I was going for help. And then I felt the pain. I tried to see who..." She shook her head. "Whoever knocked me out must have put me in the stall with Dangerous Illusion. The murderer was trying to kill me, too."

"I fear so." Exactly what he'd dreaded. Sheelin's curse simply wouldn't stop with one woman he loved. He glanced back at Dangerous Illusion, who was settling down. "Let us walk a bit. It will help clear your head."

"Bernie. He saw me..."

"Saw what?" He headed her for the open barn doors, planned on taking her straight to the SUV to get her to safety, a location where the villain couldn't find her.

"I stepped on some glass in the aisle and Bernie saw me pick it up. He had this weird expression. I didn't want to believe it..."

"Believe what?"

"It was a glass straw, Aidan. A pipette used for artificial insemination."

"What?"

"I think that's what has been going on in my barn at night. The reason George and Helen were killed. They found out about it."

To be registered as a Thoroughbred, the foal had to be a product of a live cover. Owners of most other breeds used artificial insemination with their stock, thinking it was safer with thousand-pound-plus horses, but that didn't apply to Thoroughbreds. If word got out that AI was being done at Clarke Acres, Cat's business could be ruined.

"And you think Bernie would help someone with the procedure?"

"I don't know. He never told me he was Martin Bradley's nephew, and apparently Martin has been pressuring him to do things he didn't want to do. And then there is the Jack connection. For whatever reason, my ex-husband has it in for me because I kicked him out and dared divorce him."

"Bradley has been your client all along. Do you think he would be part of a conspiracy against you?"

"I hope not, but someone used that pipette to inject a stallion's semen into a mare."

Halfway to the vehicle, Cat stopped and frowned, her expression so intent that Aidan asked, "Are you all right? Do you need help?"

"In catching a murderer." She went silent for another moment, then said, "I think I just figured things out. I know what happened and why, Aidan. But we have to prove it. The SUV." She pulled him the rest of the way. "You drive."

He'd been planning on it. But he'd also been planning on driving far enough from Woodstock to keep her safe.

"We should notify the authorities. Best to tell Detective Pierce what you think you know. Let him handle this."

"We're going to find out if I'm right first. If I am, then we'll make that call. If you don't want to come, don't."

Her tone had shifted subtly and there was a look of distrust in her beautiful hazel eyes. Knowing she would fight him if he tried to get her away from here now, Aidan nodded. As long as he didn't let her out of his sight, she would be all right. And if she really had figured it all out, they might be able to stop the villain. Or call Pierce, who would. He helped her into the SUV.

"Are you really up to this after being drugged?" he asked.

"My head is clear enough. I'm up to anything I have to do to catch a murderer."

And he was up to anything he had to do to stop a curse.

AS HER SENSE OF PURPOSE GREW, Cat felt stronger. She watched the sun sink below the horizon, and their surroundings were cast in deep shadow. "We're going around to the other side of the forest preserve, which is a bit of a ride, since there aren't many roads that go through."

Her memory also returned—all of it. Her conversation with Tim Browne about his sister Pegeen's death. Aidan's dreams. His fetching his brother from the airport. All the things he hadn't told her.

As Aidan turned onto the main road as she'd instructed, he cut into her thoughts. "Are you going to tell me where we're headed?"

"You don't like being kept in the dark. Then again, neither do I."

"You sound angry. With me?"

"Why would I be angry with you, Aidan?"

"I would not know."

"Because you've been nothing but truthful with me, isn't that right?"

Aidan went silent for a moment before asking, "What is your point, Cat?"

So here it came. Her pulse fluttered and her breath caught in her throat. But she was determined to have it all out in the open.

"Raul told me you'd hired Tim Browne to ride Mac, and I couldn't figure out why you'd hire an inexperienced jockey, so I went to see him myself. He told me he'd been a jockey for years and that he'd come to Woodstock to face you about his sister Pegeen's death. Why didn't you tell me all this on your own?"

"I would have told you. Eventually. I simply was not ready."

"Why not?" Cat choked back the threat of tears. "Because you're still in love with her? Or because you feel responsible for her death? Or is it both?"

"If you remember, I told you about Sheelin's curse on the McKennas, Cat. You did not want to believe me."

"Because I don't believe in curses. But you do. Did you dream about me, Aidan?"

Again the silence before he said, "Aye. I dreamt about your being attacked in the barn. About the needle. About your being knocked out with a drug."

"But you didn't tell me. Just like you didn't tell me about Pegeen. Or tell me about Cashel coming in from Ireland today."

"Cashel? No. 'Twas Tiernan who flew in from South Dakota."

That threw her. "Tiernan? Why?"

"To stand in for me as Mac's trainer."

"And where were you planning on being?"

"Gone. With you. I was going to take you somewhere safe until the murderer was caught."

"What?" Cat didn't even know how to respond to that. "Without asking me?"

"For your own good."

Furious with him, she sank into silence until

they got to the turnoff. How could she ever trust Aidan again?

"What happened to you is on my shoulders, Cat, and about that I am sorry."

Not responding to what she considered half an apology, she guided him to a narrow road and took him onto the farm the back way. Fewer eyes to spot them. Dusk had already settled over the farm, which was a good thing. They could be invisible in the shadows. Having only been on this property once before, she had Aidan proceed carefully and park behind a small barn set a good distance away from the other buildings.

"Let's hope there's no night staff around."

"What are we looking for?" he asked.

"You'll see in a minute."

She led the way, taking a back entrance into the barn. It was deadly quiet inside. Even so, she made no noise as she crept forward past the stalls, only three of which were occupied. Aidan shadowed her, and she had to fight not to let his nearness distract her. He'd torn her in two with his deception. She had deep feelings for him, but now she couldn't be with him again, not with so many half-truths between them.

Hearing low voices, she stopped dead in her tracks and nearly yelped when a hand covered her mouth and Aidan pulled her back into the shadows against him.

"Shh."

He removed his hand, but she was still pressed against his length. She swallowed hard and ignored the emotions being so close to him stirred up inside her. Instead, she concentrated on the voices that seemed to be moving away from them, getting softer and softer until they faded to nothing.

"They're gone."

Aidan let go of her, and she felt the separation like a physical loss.

"What are we looking for?" he asked in a whisper.

"You'll see."

The back of the barn was an open area the size of four box stalls—a large enough area for stallion sperm collection for artificial insemination. Rubber mats on the floor provided a nonslip surface. There was a door to one side, possibly the entrance to an equipment room.

She tried the handle. "Locked."

"I wish I could tell you I know how to pick a lock. It's a pretty flimsy door," he said, running his hand over it. "Seems to be nothing more than plywood. I would kick it in, but the noise might alert someone."

"A key would be easier."

Cat was already feeling above the lintel. Not

there. Nor was it under the mat on the floor before the door.

"Some farrier tools." Stooping over a box, Aidan lifted out a clinch cutter and rot shears.

"What are you going to do with those?"

He echoed her: "You'll see." Within a few minutes, he'd cut the wood around the doorknob and lifted it out. Indicating the hole that remained, he said, "My hand is too large."

Cat was able to put her hand through and unlock it from the inside. "Open Sesame."

Swinging open the door, she turned on the light and saw that she'd guessed right. Artificial insemination equipment was the proof she'd needed. She noted everything from the AV and microscope to the glass straws and syringes. Using her cell phone, she started taking photos.

"Are you going to tell me where we are now?"

"This is Dean Hill's farm."

"I was thinking it would be Bradley's after what you told me."

"I did suspect Martin and Bernie at first. I even thought maybe Jack was in on something to ruin me, too. Then when I thought about it, I allowed that Bernie just might have been shocked seeing the pipette in my hand. Suddenly it occurred to me that Martin's mares hadn't conceived yet, while Dean's conceived more quickly than normal. I thought that unusual, but I was too blind to suspect what was going on right under my nose."

"So you think Hill has been inseminating his mares as an extra measure to make sure they conceived early?"

"Or perhaps at all." Cat thought about the violence Dean had committed to keep what he was doing secret. "George must have caught him at it."

"And the vet?"

"I don't know." Cat feared Helen had somehow been involved.

"'Tis puzzling how Hill thought he could get away with using another stallion's semen, when foals are registered using DNA. They would know False Promise wasn't the stud."

"Not necessarily. Not if he had semen from a horse with matching DNA."

"Unlikely that even a full brother would match all the same markers that are tested."

"But an identical twin would." The day Aidan had arrived, they'd talked about how Memory of You had broken down as a two-year-old, before he had a chance to make a name for himself.

"So Hill kept the twin?"

"I never thought about it until now. Let's find out."

She entered the aisle where several horses were stabled. The stallion would be kept apart from the mares, so she went straight to the far end.

There he was, a blood bay with a white star on his forehead.

"I would swear that's False Promise."

She shook her head. "Nope. Take a look at his leg. The scars from the surgery after his breakdown." She pulled out her cell phone and took a couple more photos.

"So now we have proof."

"Photos. Some of that equipment with fingerprints would be better."

"Aye. Then let's fetch the evidence and get out of here."

As they headed back toward the equipment room, Aidan tried to catch hold of her, but Cat shrugged him away. No matter that he was helping her now, she wouldn't soon forget his dishonesty.

"Wear gloves so you don't get your fingerprints on the equipment."

While he slipped on a pair of latex gloves and lifted the microscope and fluid measuring tools, she went through drawers.

"We should leave."

"You go, get what you have in the SUV. I'll be right there. I'm looking to see if he kept records. If I can find them, I'll bring them."

"Don't be long."

Nothing in the drawers. If there were any

records, they had to be on computer. She heard a footfall behind her.

"What did you forget?" she asked without looking up.

"You."

Her heart lurched when she heard the voice. She whipped around to find Dean Hill blocking the doorway, an uncomfortable-looking Raul a short distance behind him.

AIDAN HAD JUST PUT THE equipment in the back of the SUV when his cell phone rang. He checked to see who was calling. The screen glowed against the dark.

Pierce.

Loving the irony, he clicked on the call. "Detective Pierce, there's been an interesting development here."

"Here, as well, McKenna. We retrieved fingerprints from the inside of the suitcase. Only problem—whoever left them doesn't have a record. No match comes up."

"Perhaps we have a match for you, along with the identity of your murderer."

Aidan quickly explained how Cat had been drugged and left to die and how she'd refused to call Pierce until she'd followed her hunch about the murderer and how they'd found the twin stallion and AI equipment.

"So Cat's hunch paid off," Aidan finished. "We're at Dean Hill's farm now."

"Get her out of there and wait someplace safe close by. I can use her expertise to explain all this equipment and such for my report. I'll call when we're within arresting distance. I'm on my way now with backup."

## *Chapter Twenty*

Abandoning any idea of deceiving Dean—Aidan's cutting the handle out of the door was wickedly obvious—Cat asked, "What were you thinking, Dean? I know you've been using artificial insemination on your mares after I bred them with False Promise. No wonder you were having such good luck."

"Luck? You think it's good luck to have a champion Thoroughbred force-retired and then, when you want to breed him, he shoots blanks? Do you realize how much money I would have lost in sales and in stud fees? How much standing in the racing community?"

"So you brought False Promise and your broodmares to my barn to do your dirty work?"

"I knew I could bribe Raul to inseminate the mares."

Cat looked over his shoulder, and to her surprise noted Raul's discomfort. She turned her focus back to Dean. "And you know that's fraud."

"Only if I'm found out." He pulled a gun from his pocket and aimed it at her. "With you gone, no one will know the difference. The DNA will be perfect. As you probably realize by now, I'm willing to do whatever it takes to make this work."

"Even murder."

"Killing George was difficult. I didn't plan it. He simply walked in on us and I couldn't let him tell anyone." With his free hand, he popped something into his mouth and chewed as he added, "Killing gets easier once you get the hang of it."

Cat wanted to be sick. This was a man who had a sterling reputation in the racing community, and he would make a fortune off his stud fees and through the sale of his foals, unless she could find a way to stop him.

"So you did mean for me to die earlier?"

"I was trying to make it look like an accident," he admitted. "Now you'll simply have to disappear like George did." He grabbed her by the arm and jerked her toward the far entrance. "Stay here, Raul, and take care of the Irishman."

Panicked at the thought of Aidan being killed because of her, Cat fought to free herself. "He never did anything to you—"

Dean jerked her silent.

"Hey, I didn't sign up for no murder," Raul protested.

"You're an accessory, Raul."

Dean kept her marching to the front of the barn. His tone verging on manic, he said, "You'll do whatever is necessary if you don't want to spend the rest of your life behind bars."

"What are you going to do with me?" Cat asked, hoping to figure a way out of whatever he had planned for her.

"After what happened to Helen, no one will think of the ravine again." He shoved her into his truck. "This time we'll dig deep enough so that no one will ever find you. You and the Irishman will simply disappear, and everyone will think you ran away together because you're the guilty ones."

He'd lost it, Cat thought, thinking there had to be a way she could use that to her advantage.

WHAT IN THE WORLD WAS taking Cat so long? Getting edgier by the second, Aidan decided to go back for her and carry her out to the SUV if need be. Pierce couldn't get here soon enough to suit him.

As he ran into the barn, he heard a vehicle speed away. He rushed to the main entrance in time to see Hill's truck drive off down the road. And Cat was in the passenger seat. His gut twisted. By the time he got to the vehicle to follow, they would be long gone.

He had to try to find them. He couldn't wait for Pierce and his backup.

But when he turned to go back, Raul stood in

his path. Aidan's hands closed into fists as he prepared to fight.

"Get out of my way!"

"You'll never catch them, not on the road—you'll be too late," Raul said to Aidan's surprise. "A horse'll get you there faster using the shortcut."

"Where?"

"The ravine. Cut around the barn straight back through the property and cross the road. When you get into the preserve, go far enough to find the trail. Keep going right."

Aidan opened the closest stall gate. "Why are you helping me instead of stopping me?" No time to tack up the mare, so he threw his leg over her bare back.

"Ain't no killer. I helped bury George because the bastard threatened to say *I* killed him. And I knocked out Miss Clarke the other night so he wouldn't kill *her*. Now he got himself another chance at her. He's lost it. He thinks he can get away with anything. You better hurry."

Already psychically connecting with the mare, Aidan felt her muscles bunch when he tangled his fingers in her mane and urged her to move off. They rounded the barn and headed straight for the back of the property.

The terrain was flat.

Smooth.

Fast.

In no time they crossed the back road, slowed to descend an incline and were surrounded by forest.

Cat filled his mind and his heart. He'd put another woman in danger. She was angry with him for holding back, but no angrier than he was with himself. His refusing to sleep with her again hadn't helped protect her. She was doomed unless he got to her in time to stop Hill.

Aidan kept the mare at an even trot as he searched out the way. Picking up the trail, he headed the mare to the right and signaled her into an easy lope until he got his bearings. Everything was pitch-dark now. The moon was a mere sliver peeking from behind a cloud. From this direction, nothing looked familiar, and he feared going too fast. He didn't want to pass the entry to the ravine.

He found it by bizarre accident—a swath of faint light fingering a stand of trees.

Aidan stopped the mare and scanned the area. The light was coming from below. The ravine. Apparently Hill had left his truck lights on so he could see what he was doing.

Praying he wasn't too late to save Cat, Aidan didn't wait to find the cleared path—he headed the mare down through the maze of trees.

DEAN HILL WAS MAKING HER dig her own grave. The only reason Cat was following orders was to stall for time.

Aidan had to be looking for her by now.

The horror of it was that Dean had moved the burial site closer to where she and Aidan had their "just sex" encounter that had sparked her feelings for him. Looking up at that very spot and remembering how exciting that had been—and then how it had all gone bad within moments when the dogs found George—she swallowed hard. No matter that she was still angry with Aidan for not being honest with her, she realized she really did love him.

To her dismay, she was starting to believe in this McKenna curse thing.

Did that mean Aidan really loved her?

Anger and disappointment didn't stop her heart from beating faster at the thought. He'd threatened to take her off somewhere until the murderer was caught. His methods might be questionable, but his heart wasn't. She'd been judging him by the mistakes she'd made in trusting and marrying Jack. Aidan wasn't anything like her ex-husband. There had to be a way to work things out between them.

If she survived.

"Keep digging!" Dean ordered. "I don't have all night."

Jamming the shovel into the rocky earth, Cat wanted to swing it smack into Dean's head. He was sitting on a tree stump several yards away, and he had that gun pointed straight at her.

"Did you make George dig his own grave before you bashed in his head?"

"He was already dead."

She just had to keep Dean off balance long enough for Aidan to find her. That shouldn't be impossible. In her opinion, Dean had already gone around the bend.

"Then I assume you made Raul do the dirty work."

"Little pissant complained about it, too. I had to threaten him, tell him I'd have the police on him." Dean laughed. "Who would believe someone like him if I said I saw him do it?"

"He had a right to complain. This is hard work. Do you know how much rock there is, considering how close we are to the stream?" To emphasize her point, she smacked her shovel against a nearby boulder.

"Don't worry, you'll have plenty time to rest. Eternity, actually." Dean laughed at his own macabre joke.

Cat eyed the water several yards away and wondered if it was deep enough to use for a getaway.

"Don't even think about it," Dean said. "I'll shoot before you get a toe wet."

Imagining she heard a soft noise that sounded like a horse blowing through its nose, her pulse surged. She said, "Tell me again why I should cooperate with you," to center Dean's attention on her.

"I have the gun, remember."

Was someone really out there? Aidan? Her spirits rose. She might survive the night, after all. She kept digging, keeping her efforts as ineffectual as possible.

"Either way you're going to kill me, right, Dean?"

"I am, but I can make it easy on you." He popped something in his mouth and chewed. "Or very, very hard. I'm getting better at this. More creative. Easy or hard…your choice."

Cat pretended to look at him, but she was subtly searching the nearby woods. "I prefer easy."

"Then dig."

Was that movement directly behind him?

Her hopes soared. She cleverly positioned herself to attack Dean. In the meantime, she had to keep him talking.

"Why didn't you bury Helen?" she asked.

"I wanted it to look like a heart attack, so no one would connect her murder to George's."

"What you did to her was gruesome—"

"It was necessary!" he yelled. "I already paid her to keep quiet about False Promise. She was my vet, too, and she's the one who determined he was sterile. When the bitch figured out I killed

George, she wanted a hundred grand to keep her mouth shut. Well, I shut it for good!"

A horse snorting made Dean jump up from the stump. As Aidan broke from the trees, Dean turned, gun arm first. Cat acted without thinking. She threw the shovel at him and ran to jump him from behind.

The second the shovel struck Dean in the middle of his back, he swung around.

"No!" Aidan shouted as the gun went off barely a yard away.

Cat jerked to a stop at the fast, sharp pain and grabbed her middle. A wet warmth covered her hands. Her head went woozy and her legs gave way.

"Cat!" Aidan yelled, as she sank to the ground.

Dean swung around again, and Cat gasped, fearing he would now shoot the man she loved.

Aidan was ready for him. He grabbed Dean's gun arm, held it high and jammed his knee into the other man's gut. Dean's grip on the gun loosened and it spun away into the dark.

Cat forced her eyes to stay open, her mind to stay in the present. Part of her wanted to drift off to someplace peaceful. Someplace without pain.

The men were still fighting, and she tried to say something that would stop them.

She couldn't find her voice. She could hardly breathe.

Dean tackled Aidan to the ground, where they rolled closer to her. They traded punches. Blood burst from Aidan's nose like a fountain, but he got his hands on the other man's neck. Dean struggled, tried to loosen Aidan's grip, but his struggle weakened.

Cat realized he would kill Dean if he didn't stop.

"Aidan, no!" Pressing her side harder to stop the bleeding, she bit back the pain. "Leave him to the law. I d-don't want to have to visit you in j-jail."

She saw her plea got through to him. He loosened his grip and Dean choked in some air.

And then the night split with whirling red lights and screaming sirens and howling dogs—Smokey and Topaz tumbled down the ravine toward her—and it felt like all hell broke loose before her world went silent.

## *Chapter Twenty-One*

"I almost killed Dean Hill," Aidan told his brother, as he waited to see Cat. She was out of surgery, out of recovery and being settled in her room. He was so grateful she'd survived that he actually felt weak with relief. "It would have been my fault, though. I nearly caused the death of another woman I love."

"You're in love." Tiernan clapped him on the back. "Congratulations, boyo."

"No congratulations required. She was almost killed. What if I can't stop it the next time?"

"Perhaps there won't be a next time," Ella said. "We've been living a peaceful and fruitful life since we got married."

"Fruitful?"

Tiernan grinned. "Ella's expecting."

"Then 'tis you two who need to be congratulated." Aidan shook his brother's hand and kissed Ella on the cheek. "But it does not change my mind that I cannot be with her."

"What about Cat's mind?" Ella asked. "Doesn't she have anything to say about it?"

Before Aidan could tell them how Cat wouldn't want him anyway because he hadn't told her about the dreams, hadn't told her about Pegeen, the nurse came out of her room.

"You can go in, now, Mr. McKenna. She's waiting for you."

"How is she?"

"She's doing fine. Go see for yourself."

Tiernan pushed him forward to the doorway.

Aidan stepped into the room and stopped where he could devour Cat with his gaze. Lying in the hospital bed, she looked so fragile. So vulnerable. He thanked his foresight in alerting Pierce, who had tracked his location through the GPS on his cell phone. Even so, there'd been a moment he'd thought it was too late, that he'd lost her. The dogs, who'd been thrown off farm property, kept off by the electric fence and so had arrived with back-up, hadn't given up on her. Neither could he.

Cat was alive.

All that mattered to him.

Her eyes fluttered open. "Aidan."

"Aye."

"Is it over?"

"All but Hill's trial. Raul made a deal with the state's attorney. He agreed to testify against Hill."

"Good. I'll testify, too."

"As will I. I shall return to see the man properly punished."

"Return?" Suddenly, she sounded anxious. "Where are you going?"

"'Tis not fair for me to take advantage of your good will any longer."

"Good will? We're partners."

"About that. I shall find a way to pay back every penny you put out to bring Mac here."

"No, you won't. We have a contract, and I'm holding you to it. You're not going anywhere without me."

Which stopped him cold. After their argument, he'd thought she would be relieved to be free of him. His pulse began to thrum.

"I put you in danger."

"What's done is done. That's the past. I'm alive and I intend to stay that way."

"You want to continue working together after all the half-truths between us? And the danger I brought you? 'Tis too big a risk."

"You take risks all the time, Aidan McKenna. With your horses. One question. No half-truths here. Are you still in love with Pegeen?"

Couldn't she see he was in love with *her?*

"I will always have room in my heart for memories of Pegeen…but at last I have put her to rest."

"Then it's time you took another risk for yourself. Take a risk on loving me."

Warmth flashed through him at the invitation. "How is it you think I love you?"

"You don't have a choice. You saved my life. It's yours."

THE DAY OF THE MCHENRY STAKES came all too soon. Out of the hospital and nearly healed, Cat held Aidan to his contract. Not that he'd tried getting out of it again, but he'd accepted her decision with a wariness that elevated her anxiety level every time she thought about it.

He hadn't admitted he loved her.

And she still was sleeping alone.

Now in the box to watch Mac race with Aidan and his brother and sister-in-law, she was both happy and envious. Tiernan's love for Ella was so obvious in the way he looked at her and touched her.

To her disappointment, Aidan seemed ill at ease, as if he wanted to say something that he couldn't force through his lips.

A declaration of love? Or was that wishful thinking?

"Mac's in the starting gate," Tiernan said.

Seeing the black colt with Tim Browne in green silks on his back, Cat felt a thrill shoot through her. She slipped her hand into Aidan's, determined to keep it there whether or not he liked it.

"This is it," she said. "The moment we've been waiting for."

"Aye."

The starting bell went off, the gates flashed open, the horses charged down the field, and Aidan squeezed her hand tightly.

People around her yelled, bettors and owners alike screaming the names of their horses.

Only Aidan wasn't yelling. Nor was Tiernan.

She looked from one brother to the other and saw the same intense expression in their rugged features, and she knew they were urging on Mac Finnian silently. Psychically.

After all that had happened, after hearing Tiernan and Ella's story, she had to believe there was something to the claim.

"C'mon, Mac!" she yelled as the field passed the half-mile post.

Browne was holding Mac back. The colt was in the middle of the field. Waiting for an opening.

And then the field entered the stretch and Mac fairly exploded past the horses on either side of him. Aidan's grip on her hand tightened even more as Mac passed the horse in front of him, then another and another until he was in second place.

Cat held her breath. The race now seemed suspended; it looked as if Mac couldn't pass the horse in the lead. And then Browne barely touched the colt's shoulder with the whip. Mac stretched out, lengthened his stride and pulled ahead. He easily took the race by two lengths.

"He won!" Cat screamed, and Aidan picked her up and twirled her around. "Mac won!"

She kissed Aidan square on the mouth and he kissed her back, hard enough to make her giddy.

When he set her down, he was smiling. "Sure and this was a sign."

"This might be only the first step, but Mac is headed for the Breeders' Cup Classic."

"A sign for us, as well," Aidan said.

Making Cat's heart thump. "What does that mean?"

"You're mine, remember?" He pulled a small box from his pocket and opened it to reveal a ring set with an emerald. "I love you, Cat Clarke. Marry me and make our partnership permanent."

"Say yes!" Ella said.

Tiernan just grinned.

Her heart soaring, Cat held out her left hand. After Aidan slipped the ring on her finger, she threw her arms around his neck and kissed him again.

Tiernan broke into their moment. "They're waiting for you in the winner's circle."

Aidan wrapped a possessive arm around her waist. "Let us go congratulate our colt."

* * * * *